∠W

ANNIE'S ATTIC MYSTERIES®

The Diary *in the* Attic

DeAnna Julie Dodson

Annie's®

AnniesFiction.com

The Diary in the Attic
Copyright © 2013, 2016 Annie's.

Library of Congress-in-Publication Data
The Diary in the Attic / by DeAnna Julie Dodson
p. cm.
I. Title
                    2012922587

AnniesFiction.com
(800) 282-6643
Annie's Attic Mysteries®
Series Editors: Ken and Janice Tate
Series Creator: Stenhouse & Associates, Ridgefield, Connecticut

10 11 12 13 14 | Printed in China | 9 8 7 6 5 4

— Prologue —

April 1943

*L*illy Pryce sat on the Lamberts' front-porch swing trying not to listen. She tried to concentrate on the touch of spring in the air and the swooping sparrows and the crocuses that poked up through the melting Maine snow and not on the voices from inside the house. Did it count as eavesdropping if she didn't understand a word they were saying? She understood the emotions behind the voices though. Peter was trying to explain, to soothe, to be logical. His mother was angry, pleading, afraid.

Lilly felt much the same way herself.

Peter was eighteen. Eighteen just today. He didn't need his mother's permission anymore. He didn't have to wait any longer.

Abruptly, the two of them were silent, and then Mrs. Lambert's voice again came through the screened front windows. Maybe it was just because it was in German, but what she said sounded terrible. Harsh. Final. There was the slam of a door, and then Peter said something else.

"Mutti."

It was still foreign, but this was soft and achingly

tender—one of the few German words Lilly did understand. *Mama.*

After that there was silence again, silence for so long that Lilly wondered if she should knock on the door and remind Peter that she was still there, or if she should quietly go back home. But she couldn't just leave. Not today.

Finally, the front door swung open, and Peter came outside.

"Sorry about that, Lil."

He gave her a bit of a smile and sat down beside her, the swing creaking with the weight of his lean, tall body. He'd look good in uniform.

She took his arm, struggling to smile in return. "What did she say?"

"Pretty much what I expected." His expression turned a little wry. "Pretty much what you said already."

"But Peter—"

"Look, they'll just draft me anyway." He thumped himself on the chest, grinning. "I'm A-1 stuff, you know."

For some reason, that brought tears to her eyes. "I know."

"Lilly, sweetheart."

"I know. I know you have to go. I'm glad you want to do your part. But this—"

"This is what I'm perfect for. Look at me."

She was looking at him. He was the picture of Hitler's Übermensch—or superman—fair skinned, blond, blue-eyed. Perfect. With his looks and background, he'd be perfect. He'd be the perfect spy.

She ought to be proud of him. She *was* proud of him.

And she was scared. Nazi Germany was a terrifying place. What they did to their own people was awful enough. What would they do to a spy if they caught him?

The tears spilled down her cheeks, and he pulled her into his arms, scrambling for his handkerchief.

"Hey, now. Hey. Nothing to cry about. They may not even want me to do anything as exotic as spying, you know. I mean, I'm still practically a kid. Maybe I'll be stuck jockeying a desk in D.C., translating intercepted enemy messages, Hess's dinner menu or something." He blotted her cheeks, his touch gentle and caressing. "And maybe while I'm there I'll meet some pretty WAVE who'll steal me away from you."

He gave her a mischievous grin, his blue eyes crinkling at the corners, and she had to laugh.

"No she wouldn't. You wouldn't let her."

"No." He cuddled her close to him, suddenly serious. "I wouldn't. Don't care where they send me, there's nobody else in the world for me but you, Lil. Nobody."

She nestled against him, her face pressed against his shoulder, breathing in the bath-soap-and-fresh-laundry smell of him. She had to let him go. It was right for him and all the other brave young men to stand up for those who could not help themselves. But if he never came back—

"Do you love me, Peter?" Her voice was soft against his neck. She wasn't sure he even heard her because he didn't answer right away.

"Just better than anything," he said at last, his voice cracking a little.

"We could—"

"No." He held her away from him so he could look into

her eyes. "We talked about this already. If the war was over, if I had a way to take care of you, you know I'd marry you in a minute. But not now. Not like this. If something were to happen to me—"

"Don't say it." She closed her eyes and the tears spilled over again. "Peter, please don't say it."

If he didn't say it, it wouldn't happen.

He pressed a tender kiss to her temple. "If I don't come back, I want you to be free."

"But I don't want to be free."

"You're only seventeen."

"I'll be eighteen this summer!"

"What if you had a kid or something, and I didn't come back? How would you provide for yourself and him?" He made her look at him again. "I love you, Lilly. I swear that's forever. But until the war is over, we'll just have to be patient."

"But, Peter, if you never—"

"Then you'll keep me in a special place in your heart, and someday, fall in love with someone else."

"No, I couldn't."

"You will." He squeezed both of her hands. "Promise me you will, Lilly."

"You wouldn't. You just told me as much."

He laughed softly. "That's me, not you. I want you to be taken care of. I want you to be happy and loved and looked after."

"What about your happiness?"

He cuddled her close again. "That would make me happy. Please, Lil, promise me."

She only clung to him, saying nothing. How could he ask her to love someone else?

"Please," he urged, and she finally nodded against his shoulder.

"I promise. But it doesn't matter. You're going to come back. You have to."

He nuzzled her cheek and then touched his lips to hers, a sweet kiss that quickly grew in intensity.

"Peter!"

Peter leapt to his feet at his mother's voice, a touch of fresh color in his face. "Ja, Mutti?"

Mrs. Lambert stood in the doorway, face pale, eyes red with weeping, but her head was held high.

"Peter," she said again, and she opened her arms to him.

He went to her, hugging her, and she said something to him in German, something that brought a look of pride into his eyes. Then she kissed his forehead and turned to Lilly with a trembling smile. Lilly came to her too, taking the hand she offered. When she spoke again, she looked to her son to translate.

Peter also smiled. "Mother says she's glad to know that, while I'm gone, someone else will be praying for me too."

Lilly nodded her assurance of that, and with a few more words of German and a firm hug for her son, Mrs. Lambert went back into the house.

Lilly looked after her and then turned to Peter. "She— she knows you're going right now? To enlist?"

He nodded. "She says my father would be proud of me, and she is too."

"But she was so upset before."

He gave her a rueful grin. "Still is. But she knows this is how it has to be. One way or another, I have to go. She knows I'd rather it be on my own terms."

He was going then. If they were smart, the Army would find a way to use his particular abilities to their best advantage. And all Lilly could do was stay home and wait for the war to be over.

"Peter, come back to me." She threw herself into his arms again. "Please come back."

He chuckled a little and kissed the top of her head. "I'm just going to the recruitment office, not Berlin, you know."

"You'll be gone soon enough." She tightened her arms around him. "Promise you'll come back."

"I will." He brought her hand to his lips and then pressed it in pledge to his heart. "I promise I will."

~ 1 ~

"Where are they?"

Annie Dawson pushed a lock of graying blond hair out of her eyes and wiped the sweat from her forehead. Then she frowned. No doubt the grime on her hand was now smeared on her face. Lovely.

She shoved aside the box she had just looked into and reached for the one next to it on the attic shelf. Gram had tons of table linens all over the house, some she had embroidered herself and some that had been given to her by friends or passed down from her own mother and grandmother. Annie distinctly remembered seeing some napkins that had little eggs and chicks and rabbits on them. They'd be perfect for the Easter banquet.

They certainly weren't in the box marked "Nancy Drew." For once, the contents of the box matched the label, and she found herself smiling at the well-loved titles. Ah, well, Nancy would have to wait for another day. Annie had linens to find.

The next box—marked "Taxes"—held a mixture of kitchen utensils, sponge rollers and Lincoln Logs. She found three boxes full of encyclopedias that looked like they were from about 1920 and a suitcase full of women's clothes that looked like they were even older than that. Behind that was a case with a fine set of woodworking tools, and behind that was a box marked "Lilly."

Annie pulled the box down and set it on top of an old chest. She couldn't remember if Gram had ever mentioned a Lilly before. Gram had known just about everybody in Stony Point and had so many friends. But who was Lilly?

There wasn't all that much in the box. There was a scratched-up, old seventy-eight rpm record of The Andrews Sisters' *Don't Sit Under the Apple Tree (With Anyone Else but Me)*. A collector might love it, but she knew hardly anyone who still had a turntable these days, much less one that would play seventy-eights. The box also held a stack of letters, some of them extremely small, a few photos, and a little silver ring in the shape of a lover's knot. Under everything else was a red-leather diary with "1943" embossed in gold on the front and a tiny key on a string.

She unlocked the book and opened it. On the first page, on the printed line under "THIS DIARY BELONGS TO," the name *Lillian Eileen Pryce* was written in faded blue ink with a fountain pen. Annie could tell by little blots of ink where the letters started and stopped, and where each "I" was dotted.

Annie turned the page, yellowed with age, the gilded edges tarnished. January first. She smiled at the very first words. *He kissed me.*

It was too terribly sweet, and she couldn't help wondering again who Lillian was, how Gram had known her, and where she was now. Curious, Annie read on.

He kissed me. Just at the stroke of twelve, Peter Lambert kissed me. Daddy would have a fit if he knew, but it was New Year's Eve after all, and Peter and I have known each other since we were kids. I don't think he'd really mind if he'd seen how sweet Peter was. Not pushy like some other boys try to be. But I'm glad this diary has a lock on it anyway.

1943. Even if this Lillian had been a teenager back then, she'd be very old now. Eighty-something at least. Probably passed on. Still, it was sweet. Then or now, teenage girls were teenage girls. Still grinning, Annie rummaged through the box again. This time she took out the pictures. One of them had to be of Lillian.

The first picture, though, was definitely not Lillian. It showed a young man in the uniform of an Army private. He was standing on the front porch of a house, leaning against one of the posts, looking as if he was trying not to laugh. The picture was black and white, of course. Not the sepia of photos from earlier eras, but the steely black and white of the 1940s. His hair and eyes looked light. Very likely he was blond haired and blue-eyed. And if this was Peter Lambert, it was no wonder Lillian hadn't minded him kissing her. He was remarkably handsome.

And young. Annie sighed. Very, very young to be sent into a war halfway around the world. Had he made it home again?

She looked at the next picture. It was of the same boy, she thought, even though she had very little to base that on. She had read only a part of Lillian's diary entry from January first. However, if she was a typical teen, by March Lillian could have been raving over another boy. In fact, this young soldier might be someone entirely different.

In this second photograph, the boy was seated on a floral couch with his arm around an older woman—his mother, Annie assumed from the similarities in their features. He was again in uniform, but this time he looked more somber, and he was looking up at the camera as if the photographer had taken him by surprise. The woman, too, looked startled, and the hand she used to clutch the boy's arm had a handkerchief wadded up in it. Somehow, this picture made Annie want to cry. Was this taken during a last visit home before he was shipped overseas?

There were several other pictures in the box, all of them of the same boy. In some he wore his civilian clothes, dungarees and flannel shirts, or Sunday-best suits, and he looked a bit younger than in the uniformed ones. But there were none where he looked older. *Had he ever come home again?* Annie wondered.

Well, she wasn't going to keep on assuming that this was Peter Lambert if, by sometime in February, Lillian was gushing about a Joey or a Sam or a Robert. Just to make sure, Annie opened the diary to the middle of April.

He wouldn't let me go with him to the recruiting office. I don't know why, but he said it's something a man has to do on his own. I guess he didn't care that he just dumped me off at home. Oh, Peter, if you don't come back to me, I'll never speak to you again!

Annie didn't know if she wanted to laugh or cry. Obviously the girl had been too upset to realize the incongruity of that statement. Poor thing. Annie was glad she hadn't had to see Wayne go off to war. It had been hard enough losing him when she did, but at least they had had a good life together before that. They'd had a daughter and eventually, grandchildren. It was time for which Annie would be forever thankful. She couldn't even imagine how terrible it would have been to lose him before they could even start their marriage.

She closed the diary and opened one of the letters. It was dated November 12, 1943, and she smiled to see the holes the censors had cut in it. The salutation was, "Lilly darling." So Lillian went by Lilly.

Lilly darling,

I'm not allowed to say where I am or where I'm going, but the weather is --------- for two days. I'm sorry I won't be able to write often, but in my line of work, that wouldn't be too smart. Besides, anything I can write home about would be pretty dull anyway. Someday, when we're old and gray, I'll tell you all my hair-raising adventures. But don't you worry about me, even if it's a long while between letters. I'll write whenever it's safe and when I'm someplace that will get my letters over stateside. I'm real sorry I can't get mail very often either, and that will probably get worse too, but it's sure like Christmas when I do. Between you and my mother, I don't know anybody who gets as many letters as me. When I was in ---------------- 23 of them! I hope you can keep sending me the write ups on the hockey games. I sure miss being on the team. Don't stop writing me, even if you don't hear back for a long time. You don't know how much your letters keep me going over here. How much they remind me just what I'm fighting for and what I'm coming home to. Someday, darling. And you'd better be staying out from under that apple tree!

Love always,
Peter
PS—Saw your old beau Jimmy a couple of weeks ago. He

was on the ---------- that brought me over to ----------- and asked about you. I told him you were strictly hands off, or I'd knock his block off.

Annie smiled and put the letter back into its envelope. Then she picked up another, this one dated November 30, 1943.

Lilly darling,
I miss you more than I can say, and I may not be able to write you again for a long time. I can't tell you anything about where and when I'm going, but I need you to keep me in your prayers. Don't worry. Just pray. And remember your promise. I'm remembering mine.
Love always,
Peter
PS—Please go see my mother if you have time. I know you can't really talk to her, but if you could just go see her, I know it would help. Maybe Bessie can go with you to translate. Thanks, sweetheart.

"Hey, Annie, you still up there? Did you find them?"

Startled back into the present, Annie slipped the letters and the diary back into the box. "Coming, Alice!"

Annie hurried down the attic steps and into the kitchen where her next-door neighbor and best friend, Alice MacFarlane, was sitting at the table drinking coffee. Alice laughed, her bright blue eyes sparkling.

"I don't see any linens, but whatever you did find up there must have been awfully grubby."

Annie grinned and went to the kitchen sink to wash her hands and face. "It never fails to amaze me to see everything Gram squirreled away up there."

Alice nodded wisely. "I think she had just as wide a range of friends."

"She sure did." Annie poured herself a fresh cup of coffee and sat down across from Alice. "You don't remember Gram knowing someone named Lilly, do you?"

"No. Lilly who?"

"Pryce. Sound familiar?"

Alice shook her head. "Why?"

"I found a box of her things up there—all from the Second World War. Letters and a diary and things."

"Ah. I was wondering what kept you so long."

"Sorry about that." Annie gave her friend a sheepish grin. "I got a little distracted. I think this Lilly must have been about Gram's age. Maybe three or four years younger, but probably not much."

"So what was so interesting?" Alice asked.

"I guess it was like just about everybody during the war. She stayed behind while her sweetheart was off fighting. They were just so ... young."

Alice sighed. "I suppose it's been that way as long as there have been wars—and that's been forever."

"I suppose." Annie sighed too. "Oh, well, I guess finding out what happened to Lilly and her boyfriend won't help us get this banquet planned. I never did find the linens I was hoping we might use."

"Right." Alice pulled her open spiral notebook over in front of her and tapped the half-filled page with her ballpoint pen. "OK, before we were distracted by which linens we should use, we were talking about seeing what we could do to include people who don't usually come to our church."

"Well, you know a lot of people come on Easter Sunday even if they don't come any other day of the year."

"Right."

"We need to make sure they know they're welcome to the banquet too. And not just them." Annie thought again about Lilly, and what her life might be like if she was still alive. "There are a lot of people, especially older people, who don't have anyone to take them to church or have lunch with them afterwards. I'm thinking we should make a special effort to invite those people and give them transportation to and from the event. What do you think?"

Alice nodded. "That's a great idea. You know, I'm wondering if we could even invite some of the folks from our assisted-living facilities over—the ones who are able to come, of course. I know a lot of them don't have very many visitors or have a chance to get out much. You think we could manage something like that?"

"Absolutely!" Annie gave her friend's arm a squeeze. "I think it's a wonderful idea. Of course, we'll have to talk it over with the other ladies on the committee when they get here, but it's a lovely idea."

"Good. Then there's the Easter egg hunt. I suppose if the weather is bad, we could have that in the fellowship hall."

"I suppose, but that's not nearly as fun as outside," Annie said, "and there aren't many good places to hide the eggs."

"We could always—"

The doorbell rang, and Annie stood up. "Hold that thought until everybody is settled in."

She opened the door, smiling to see Mary Beth Brock and Kate Stevens on her front porch. "Come in! Come in!"

"Thanks for having us, Annie," Kate said, her dark eyes warm. "I love being in Grey Gables. It always reminds me of Betsy."

Annie's inheritance of Grey Gables from her grandmother, Elizabeth Holden, had led her back to Stony Point, Maine's scenic coastline. The stately Victorian-era home was the site of many of Annie's favorite times of childhood, the place where she often summered with her grandparents while her missionary parents were overseas. It was there she had first met Alice, developing a friendship that spanned their teenage years and then was rekindled when Annie returned to Maine after Betsy's death.

Mary Beth Brock was the owner of A Stitch in Time, Stony Point's needlecraft shop, and Kate Stevens worked in the store. Kate was also becoming widely known for her crochet pattern designs.

Annie gave Kate a brief hug. "You're more than welcome. That's a gorgeous sweater. I suppose that's one of your own designs?"

Kate looked down, pink-cheeked and smiling, but Mary Beth nodded and modeled her own crocheted cardigan.

"This one too. Isn't it delicious? I'll have both patterns for sale at the shop by next week." She chuckled. "I love Kate's patterns because they look good even on those of us who are—ahem—less than svelte."

Annie and Kate giggled, and the three women went back

into the kitchen. A few minutes later, Peggy Carson and Gwendolyn Palmer joined them around the kitchen table.

Peggy, a waitress at The Cup & Saucer, clasped her plump hands in front of her. "All we need is Stella, and we might as well have a Hook and Needle Club meeting right here." She was the youngest and most exuberant member of the club.

"I think Reverend Wallace has figured out that if he wants to get something done, he can call on us," Alice said. "We'll tackle it with a vengeance."

"He's such a dear," Gwen said. "It's nice to be able to give him some help once in a while." Gwen, the group's most prominent socialite, was the wife of John Palmer, the president of Stony Point Savings Bank. She always was ready to embrace a new challenge.

Annie smiled. "Alice and I were thinking it might be nice to have some of the folks come over from Seaside Hills and Ocean View to the church service and then to the banquet on Easter. What do the rest of you think?"

"It's a great idea," Peggy said, "but how will they all get there?"

"When Mom was at Seaside, they had vans they used for outings," Mary Beth said as she got up to pour herself another cup of coffee. "I'm sure it's the same at Ocean View."

"We'd have to clear this with both places of course," Alice said. "But I don't know why they'd object. We'll check it out." She turned to the next topic. "Now, about the egg hunt, if the weather's bad, and we have to—"

Annie chuckled as the doorbell again interrupted Alice. "That'll be Stella. Be right back."

Stella Brickson smiled wistfully when Annie opened the

door. Stella, the matriarch of the Hook and Needle Club, had been Betsy Holden's close childhood friend.

"You know, I still almost expect Betsy to answer that door when I come to Grey Gables."

"I'm sure Gram would be so glad to know that," Annie said, squeezing Stella's shoulder and drawing her inside, "and she would be glad to know that you and I are friends too."

With a twinkle in her eye, Stella took Annie's arm, and they went to join the others in the kitchen. Stella sat at the head of the table and pulled a skein of variegated blue yarn and a pair of knitting needles from her tote bag and began to cast on. "So what have we decided?"

"Not much yet," Alice told her. "Annie *didn't* find Betsy's Easter table linens up in the attic, but we did discuss bringing some of the residents from Seaside Hills and Ocean View out to the church service and then to the banquet."

Annie brought Stella a cup of coffee and then sat down. "That reminds me, Stella. Did you ever know a Lilly Pryce? I know she lived in Stony Point in 1943 because that's how her letters were addressed, but I don't know much more than that."

"Hmmm." Stella's needles paused in their methodical clicking for a moment. "There were some Pryces who lived a few streets over from us back then, but they moved sometime after the war. I didn't really know them, though I'm sure there was a daughter. Could've been Lilly, but that was so long ago. Why?"

"Annie's working on another of her mysteries. Lost lovers this time." Alice grinned. "And all this while she's been trying to convince us she's immune to romance."

Annie rolled her eyes. "I just found a diary and some letters, that's all."

"Ooh, love letters?" Peggy leaned forward in her seat, her round face alight. "Tell! Tell!"

Annie's mouth turned up at the corners. "Well, from what I saw—and really, I only had a minute to look at the stuff—Lilly must have been about sixteen or seventeen and she had a boyfriend who was sent overseas. From one of the letters he sent her, it sounds like he might have been assigned to something pretty secret—maybe espionage or something like that, though it's hard to tell by what he wrote and what the censors let get through. I'm just curious about what happened to them."

"Like I said," Alice concluded, "another mystery."

"I remember when John was drafted for Vietnam," Gwen said softly. "I was so afraid for him."

Mary Beth gave her a sympathetic smile. "I remember those days."

"If you're going to talk to the people at the retirement homes about the banquet," Stella said, "you might as well see if anyone over there remembers your Lilly Pryce."

"Oh, Stella, that's brilliant!" Annie beamed at her. "Absolutely brilliant."

Stella only lifted one silver eyebrow and kept her attention on her knitting. "Don't sound so surprised."

*   *   *   *

The next day, Annie and Alice went to talk to Susan Rigsby, the activity director at Seaside Hills Assisted Living, to discuss inviting their residents to the Easter service and banquet. Mrs. Rigsby seemed glad to give her charges a break from their usual routine and was eager to help.

"By the way, Mrs. Rigsby," Annie said as she escorted them back through the corridor toward the exit, "I was wondering if you have anyone here who might remember Stony Point during World War II."

Mrs. Rigsby smiled. "Oh, several, I'm sure. Is there something specific you'd like to know?"

"I'm trying to find someone who might have known a Lilly Pryce."

"Miss?"

Annie turned at the soft voice from behind her.

"I know Lilly."

2

"*I* know Lilly," the woman repeated.

Annie turned to see a frail-looking woman in a wheelchair. Her body was wizened and tiny, but her black eyes were bright, and there was a smile on her quivering lips.

"Hello," Annie said, smiling back. "I'm looking for Lilly Pryce. Is she here?"

Mrs. Rigsby shook her head. "No, we definitely don't have anyone by that name with us now. I don't recall ever having anyone called Pryce, but I'd have to check the records to be sure. Do you know a Lilly Pryce, Mrs. Madison?"

The woman in the wheelchair frowned, thinking. "I know Lilly. She stayed here for a while, but she's gone now."

"She passed away?" Annie asked as gently as she could, but the woman shook her head.

"No, she got her own apartment. Her shoulder used to bother her, but after she had therapy for a while, she moved out. We still visit sometimes."

Annie smiled, liking that outcome much better. "Is her name Lilly Pryce?"

"No, not Pryce. It's Lilly Bergstrom. But she said she lived over on Oak Lane when she was growing up here in Stony Point. I didn't know any Bergstroms lived there. Maybe I'm just not remembering right."

Annie glanced at Alice and then back at Mrs. Madison. "Is Lilly Bergstrom's apartment in Stony Point?"

"I don't know. I don't think it's very far, but since I don't drive, I just don't pay much attention. My daughter or my granddaughter takes me. Mostly Lilly comes here anyway."

Annie smiled at Mrs. Madison once more. "Do you remember if she ever got a visit from Betsy Holden when she was here?"

Mrs. Madison beamed at her. "Oh, I remember Betsy. She made the most beautiful crocheted sweaters. She gave Lilly a cross-stitched bookmark with a Bible verse on it. Prettiest one I ever saw."

"Betsy was my grandmother. I know she had a lot of friends here at Seaside. Did she visit with Lilly Bergstrom?"

"Oh, yes. Several times, I think."

"Do you think this Lilly Bergstrom is the Lilly you're looking for, Annie?" Alice asked softly.

"I suppose she could be. I know she lived on Oak Lane from the address on Peter's letters to her. Mrs. Rigsby, do you have a current address for her?"

Mrs. Rigsby shook her head. "I'm sorry, but we're not allowed to give out any kind of information like that. Federal regulations, you know."

Alice grinned. "Maybe we just need to look her up in the phone book."

*   *   *   *

"It's easy when you know how, huh?" Alice grinned and pointed to the listing for L.P. Bergstrom in the phone book.

"It's those apartments on Shore Road off Highway 32 in Bremen, apartment 402."

"Hmmm," Annie mused. "L.P.? Lilly Pryce?"

"A lot of older ladies living alone use initials," Alice said. "It's worth a shot." She gave Annie's arm a playful push. "Go on. You know you want to."

Annie punched the number into her cellphone, feeling a little excited, apprehension skittering through her veins. Could it really be Lilly? The Lilly who wrote the diary?

On the third ring, someone picked up. "Hello?"

Annie's heart fluttered. "Hello. Is this Mrs. Lilly Bergstrom?"

"Yes. What can I do for you?"

Mrs. Bergstrom's voice was low and soft with only a touch of the Maine accent that Annie had grown used to again over the past few years.

"I'm sorry to bother you, Mrs. Bergstrom, but my name is Annie Dawson. I think you might have known my grandmother, Betsy Holden."

"Oh, yes." Mrs. Bergstrom's voice was suddenly infused with warmth. "And I remember her talking about her granddaughter, Annie. Goodness. I can't believe it's already been more than four years since she left us. You must miss her terribly."

"Yes, ma'am, I do," Annie admitted. "In a roundabout way, it's because of her that I'm calling you. May I ask if your maiden name is Pryce?"

"Why, yes. Yes, it is. How did you know?"

Annie looked over at Alice and nodded, grinning broadly. "Do you think it would be OK if I stopped by to talk to you for just a few minutes? I know that's not much notice."

"Oh, sure," Mrs. Bergstrom said. "I was just watching an old movie, but my DVD player's pause button is in fine working order."

Annie chuckled. "I don't want to interrupt you."

"No, really, it's fine. I've seen it many times. I'm sure that wicked Basil Rathbone will still get what's coming to him."

"Is now OK?" Annie asked, still grinning. "I'm just leaving Seaside Hills. There was a lady—Mrs. Madison—who told me she remembered you."

"Well, come on! I'd love to talk to you about Betsy."

Once she had confirmed the address and got directions on how to get there, Annie thanked her and hung up the phone.

"It's her. It's Lilly. I can hardly believe it."

"Hmmm, I guess it makes sense that she would live nearby." Alice wrinkled her forehead. "I wonder why Betsy had her things though—especially something as personal as a diary."

"I guess we'll find out, huh? Or would you rather I dropped you back home before I go? If you have something—"

"Oh, no." Alice grinned. "I think your Lilly has a story, and I want to know what it is."

*   *   *   *

It took Annie and Alice only a few minutes to get to Lilly's apartment. The building was situated just off the highway and couldn't have been more than five or six years old. It was nothing fancy, but it was nice and well maintained. It was probably quite pretty in the summer when the trees leafed out and there were ducks in the pond. A banner over the leasing office said "Gracious Retirement Living."

"Here we are," Annie announced as she pulled her beloved Chevy Malibu—a gift from her late husband, Wayne—into an empty parking space. "That's hers. Right over there."

Annie tapped the knocker just below the plaque that said "402," grinning at Alice in anticipation. Soon the door opened, and Annie smiled.

"Mrs. Bergstrom?"

"Yes. And you must be Annie."

She was a small woman, her white hair in a stylish short cut and her brown eyes still appealingly doe-like. She wore a comfortable-looking pink warm-up suit, a fluffy white sweater, and a string of pearls. Added to that was a flattering touch of lipstick and a hint of perfume.

Lilly looked uncertain when Annie only stood smiling at her. "Won't you come in?"

Annie glanced at Alice and then again at Lilly. "Thank you. And thank you for letting us drop by on such short notice, Lilly. Oh, excuse me—I mean, Mrs. Bergstrom."

"No, no, honey, you call me Lilly. 'Mrs. Bergstrom' makes me sound like an old lady."

Her brown eyes sparkled, and Annie had to laugh.

"Thank you, Lilly. I'm sorry for staring, but I—well, I'm still a little bit amazed to find you here. I mean, so close to Stony Point," Annie said. "Oh, excuse me. This is my friend, Alice MacFarlane. She lives next door to Grey Gables. Alice and I knew each other when we were both kids and I would visit Gram during the summer. When Gram passed, she bequeathed Grey Gables to me."

Alice smiled too. "Hi. It's good to meet you, Lilly."

"Hello, Alice," Lilly said. "Come in, both of you, and make yourselves comfortable."

Thanking her, Annie and Alice stepped into the apartment. It was all light and air, decorated in delicate creams and yellows and lovely floral prints. Their eyes widened as they noticed the intricate cross-stitch masterpieces hung on the walls.

"Oh, my." Alice came close to one, a glorious rendition of John Waterhouse's classic painting, *Penelope and the Suitors*, and her mouth fell open. "This is wonderful."

"Amazing," Annie agreed, and then she smiled at Lilly. "Did you do this?"

"Yes." There was a touch of color in Lilly's cheeks. "Took me quite a while too, but I must confess I'm rather proud of it."

"Alice is a cross-stitcher too," Annie said, and Alice laughed and shook her head.

"I don't think I can call myself that anymore. Not after seeing your work." Alice wandered over to an intricate floral piece hung above the couch. "These are all just stunning."

"That's one of Betsy's designs," Lilly told them, and Annie nodded.

"I can tell. You did it beautifully."

Lilly sighed. "I miss it now. Betsy and I had some wonderful talks over our stitching, I can tell you. I miss her too."

"Don't you cross-stitch anymore?" Alice asked.

"No. I'm afraid I have just enough arthritis in my hands to keep me away from it. Ah, well, at least I still have all these." Lilly sat on the cream-color couch and invited the other two to join her. "Now, how can I help you? I can't believe I'm finally getting to meet little Annie. Your grandmother spoke of you so often."

"Well, if you knew Gram at all, you must have known what a pack rat she was."

"Don't I remember!" Lilly laughed. "Good thing she had that big, old house. No telling what all she had in there."

Alice grinned at her. "That's what we came to talk to you about."

"You gave Gram some things to keep for you, didn't you?" Annie asked.

Lilly smiled wistfully. "Just a few old memories I wasn't ready to throw out. I suppose I should have, but I couldn't quite do it. I had to get rid of a lot of things when I sold my house and went to stay at Seaside for a while. I fell and hurt my shoulder and had to have surgery. I knew I was going to need help and therapy for several months. My son wanted me to come stay with him, but his wife's aunt already lives with them, and I thought that might make things a little awkward—you know? So once I left Seaside, I came here. I didn't really need a big house all by myself anyway. But that was after Betsy died. I figured all that stuff I left with her had been thrown out. Are you telling me it's still there?"

Annie smiled at the eager hopefulness in the older lady's eyes. "Still there. I came across a box containing your things the other day, and I wanted to see if I could find you."

Lilly beamed at her. "I can't believe it's still there. I'm so glad it wasn't thrown out. Betsy was a dear to hang on to it for me."

"I'm sure Gram was happy to help you out," Annie

assured her. "But I was wondering if you'd tell me about all those things." She felt a little bit awkward now. Suddenly those letters and pictures and the diary weren't just souvenirs of a time long past. They were this lady's private hopes and dreams and fears—her cherished memories—something too precious to her to be discarded even after all this time.

"I'm sorry." Annie winced slightly. "I think I should apologize for reading those things without your permission."

"You didn't even know I was alive when you did, honey. Not too many of us left from back then you know. I would have done the same thing." Lilly took her arm. "It's sweet of you to even ask about all of it. Do you really want to know about Peter?"

3

"Annie's favorite hobby is solving other people's mysteries," Alice said with a laugh. "Of course she wants to know about Peter."

Annie looked at Lilly with a warm smile. "If it doesn't bother you to talk about him, I would love to know."

The older woman's eyes were shining and wistful. "I haven't told anyone about Peter in years and years. Not since before I got married. If you don't mind hearing me ramble on, I'd love to tell you." She made an impatient little sound. "Forgive me. Would either of you like some coffee? I'm about to get some for myself."

"May I get it?" Alice offered. "I hate to trouble you."

"Oh, sure, honey." Lilly indicated the efficient little kitchen on the other side of the living room. "It's already made. Cups are in the cabinet above the coffeemaker. Cream's in the fridge, and sugar's on the counter."

"Can I help?" Annie asked, but Alice only shook her head, already in the kitchen.

"You two go ahead. Just talk loud enough for me to hear. What do you take in yours, Lilly?"

"A spoon of sugar and some cream, thank you." Lilly turned to Annie. "So you came across that box of things I left with Betsy. I guess I could have asked my son to hold onto all that for me, but ... well, I don't know if he would have really understood why I kept it for all these years. Most likely I shouldn't have once I married his father. But I just couldn't toss Peter away like that. There was something special about him."

"He was certainly handsome," Alice said from the kitchen. "I saw the pictures."

"I'd love to see them again." A glow came into Lilly's dark eyes. "Peter could have gone to Hollywood if he'd wanted to, he was that good-looking. I always thought he was built like Errol Flynn in his prime—tall and lean and sleekly muscled, you know? Besides that, there was just something about him that turned heads. But he was never one for a lot of attention. I remember when we were in high school, and he played the part of Prince Charming in the school play. He looked truly magnificent in doublet and hose and a crown—like a real prince—but he was terribly embarrassed. The other boys teased him mercilessly, but they were just jealous. Kitty Bender, the girl who played the princess, was a tall girl, and none of the other boys were tall enough for her." She winked. "At least none of the good-looking ones."

Annie chuckled. "Sounds like he was a good sport about it."

"Mrs. Hildebrandt, the English teacher, was in charge of the play that year. She convinced him it just couldn't be done without him. Peter was so softhearted, he just couldn't tell her no." Lilly sighed, smiling still. "I suppose it's easy, looking back, to remember him a little more perfect than he was. He could be stubborn when he wanted to be and more than a little too protective. But he meant well, and he was never one to shirk a responsibility or forget a promise."

"I have to know," Annie said as gently as she was able. "Did he come home? All those pictures of him, he looks so young."

Lilly shook her head, something wistful and sad in her slight smile. "He was eighteen. Just eighteen when he enlisted. It was his birthday, in fact. His poor mother—"

"I can imagine it must have been awful for her."

"No, he never came home. He shipped out in the summer of 1943, after boot camp. Before Christmas, we got word that he had been killed."

Annie gave her hand a sympathetic little squeeze.

"Of course, they never said killed," Lilly said, squeezing back. "They said missing. It was so hard not knowing for certain. I tried to keep hoping, even though the Army obviously thought he was dead. Eventually, I had to stop believing in fairy tales." She smiled again, determinedly cheerful. "Life goes on."

"What happened to him?" Alice asked as she set their coffee on the table and then sat down herself.

"They never told us, and even after all these years, I can't help wondering about him. Knowing Peter, he went out like a hero, single-handedly saving his platoon, or smuggling Jewish children into England, or something insanely brave like that. He never liked bullies, and for him, Hitler was nothing more than the worst kind of bully."

"Those times must have been scary." Annie shook her head. "Not that today isn't a little unnerving at times too."

"It wasn't so bad for those of us who stayed at home," Lilly said. "Of course we had rationing and shortages of all kinds. But it was nice to see the country pulling together.

And it showed us what we could do when we put our minds to it. It was the people overseas who had an awful time of it—our soldiers, of course, and the poor people who lived in Europe and Asia and the Pacific. The English people almost starved to death. And the Germans, just the everyday people, I think it may have been the worst for them. Talk about a frightening place to live during the war. And we didn't know much about what was happening over there at the time."

"Did you ever wonder if the war would come to the States?" Alice asked.

Lilly nodded and took a sip of her coffee. "I think that's why a lot of our men were eager to get into the Army and the Navy. Better to take care of things over there before it had a chance to come here."

Annie gave her a sympathetic smile. "Still, it must have been hard to see them go. Especially knowing so many of them would never come back."

Lilly's doe-brown eyes filled with sadness as fresh as it must have been seventy years earlier. "They were so brave. I suppose they didn't really know what they would be facing. Not most of them. So many of them were just boys really; many had never been away from home before. At least Peter had been overseas a few times when he was younger."

"Had he?" Annie asked, encouraging her to go on.

"Oh, yes. His parents were German," Lilly explained. "From somewhere not far from Berlin—Potsdam, I believe. His poor mother never spoke English at all, you know, even though she and her husband came to America after the First World War, before Peter was born. He was raised speaking nothing but German at home. On top of that, he visited family in Germany many times before his father died—before things got bad over there—so he knew the country and the people as well as the language. I guess in a lot of ways he was still such a boy. He wanted to do big things to help the war effort, and he thought he was particularly suited to do some kind of undercover work. And, really, he was. With his looks and background, he was perfect." Lilly shook her head. "I guess the Army must have thought so too. Once he got out of boot camp, he came home for a few days on leave. That was the last time I saw him."

"Is that picture of him—the one on the couch—from that leave?" Annie asked. "I guessed that is his mother next to him, but I wasn't sure."

"I think I know the one you mean. Yes, if it's an older lady sitting beside him, that's his mother." Lilly laughed softly. "'Older lady.' She was probably about half my age now when that was taken. Poor thing."

Annie squeezed her hand. "She must have taken it hard when she got the news that he was killed."

*   *   *   *

December 1943

Lilly stood on tiptoe, draping silver garland on the freshly cut pine tree that now stood in her front room. They usually went out into the woods together, she and Mom and Daddy, and cut one themselves, but Mom had her hands full working with the other ladies, still packing up Christmas bundles to go to the boys overseas, and Dad was working extra hours at the mill as it ran through twenty-four–hour days, turning out cloth for uniforms.

On the day after Thanksgiving, they usually made quite an occasion of putting up the tree, but now December was half over, and it hadn't been done. So Lilly had bribed a couple of neighbor boys with cookies and sweet talk to help her bring home and set up the tree she bought, and now it stood sparkling with lights and gleaming with tinsel and the delicate glass ornaments passed down from her grandmother. She had draped some garland on the mantel too, and set out the prettiest of the Christmas cards they had received. It would all look beautiful tonight under the glow of the hearth fire—the perfect picture of a cozy, peaceful Christmas at home.

This would have been my first real Christmas with Peter, Lilly thought.

She bit her lip at the thought and blinked back tears. It didn't do any good to cry over it now. He wasn't going to be home this Christmas. Maybe he wouldn't be home for the next one or the next. Maybe he wouldn't—

No, she wouldn't let herself think more than that. He had promised he'd come home. He would come home. When the war was over, when he'd done what he could to serve the cause of freedom, he'd come home. There would be more Christmases than just this one. They were young. They had time.

"Oh, Peter, please come home," she whispered. "Please come home to me. Please—"

A rapid knock on the door made her drop the empty packing box she held. The wild idea that he could be out there on her front porch, come home to surprise her, made her heart pound a little more quickly as she hurried to answer the door. She had heard stories like that from other girls who had sweethearts in the service, and her hand trembled as she turned the knob. *Oh, please—*

She smiled wanly to see a little girl in a too-snug red woolen coat, her mousy brown hair in two untidy braids.

"Bessie!"

"I'm sorry, Lilly. Can I come in for a little bit?" Bessie's eyes were wide, and she looked as if she would burst into tears any minute.

"Sure. Come in and get warm. Are you OK?"

She nodded and hurried inside, going to stand for a moment by the fire. "I—I don't know if I'm supposed to tell, but—oh, Lilly."

Now she did start to cry, and Lilly gave her a handkerchief. "What is it, honey? What's wrong?"

"Mutti—" She hiccuped and started again. "Mutti got a telephone call from Frau Lambert a little while ago."

Lilly nodded. Like Peter, Bessie Opitz was the American-born child of German parents. She, too, spoke only German at home, and her parents, as well as some of the other German natives in the neighborhood often asked her to serve as translator. No doubt she had been exposed to things that no ten-year-old should know about, but she was a good girl and not one to gossip about the information she was entrusted with.

"Mutti says I'm never supposed to tell anyone about any translating I do, but I think you have to know."

"What is it, honey? Is something wrong with Mrs.

Lambert?" Lilly knelt down to have her eyes level with the little girl's. "What is it?"

"She—She got a wire from the Army. Peter—Peter—"

Lilly's fingers tightened on the little red coat as tears spilled down the girl's rounded cheeks. Poor, dear Bessie. She had a sweet, little-girl crush on Peter, and Peter—

Please go see my mother if you have time. She remembered the words from his last letter. *I know you can't really talk to her, but if you could just go see her, I know it would help.*

Lilly swallowed hard and stood up. She wouldn't cry. She wouldn't.

She took the handkerchief from Bessie and swiftly blotted the little girl's face. Then she put on her own coat and took the girl's hand.

"Come on, sweetie. Your mother will be worried about you."

She walked the two blocks to Bessie's house, not looking at the girl, knowing she was crying the whole time. Once she saw her safely to her own door, she hurried to Peter's house.

When she turned up the walk, she saw Mrs. Lambert standing in the front window, clutching the curtain in one hand and a paper of some kind in the other. She was at the door before Lilly could knock.

"Lilly!"

Sobbing out a broken torrent of German, the older woman pulled Lilly inside and sat down with her on the sofa. She held out the paper in her hand. A telegram. *The* telegram.

"Peter," she managed to say. "Peter."

Lilly took the telegram, scanning it for the only words that mattered. *Missing. Believed killed.*

And then she took Peter's mother into her arms and wept.

*   *   *   *

"We never did get any details about what happened to him. And poor little Bessie." There were tears in Lilly's eyes. "She shouldn't have had to carry that kind of news. She was hardly more than a baby."

Annie wanted to cry herself to think of Lilly at seventeen having to be told the boy she loved was gone. And yet she was no different from thousands upon thousands of other girls, other women, who had sent their men to war and had never seen them come home again. And all the mothers—

"What did Mrs. Lambert do after the war?"

"It was terribly sad." Lilly put her hand over Annie's. "She died right before Christmas the next year. They said it was a gas leak in her house, but I always wondered. I ... I guess she was a little lost without Peter. Once her husband died, Peter pretty much took care of everything for her. And then she lost him too, and so very young. I always felt bad for her."

"Oh, how awful," Alice murmured, looking into her nearly empty cup.

"I tried to convince myself that he was only missing," Lilly said. "I tried to tell myself he wasn't really dead. But when the war ended, and he didn't come home, I knew I had to stop kidding myself."

Annie shook her head. "And you never knew what happened to him? The War Department didn't ever give you any details about what he was doing or why he was believed killed?"

"No. I got a letter from him, the very last one, where he told me I might not hear from him for a long time. He said—" Lilly pressed her trembling lips together and managed a smile. "He said I shouldn't worry. Just pray for him."

"I think I saw that one. And you never heard from him again?"

"Never." Lilly sighed. "I'm sure he must have been assigned to some sort of espionage—like he always wanted—and they kept all that information secret. I did pray. For the longest time, I prayed and prayed, but I never heard anything else. I never knew what happened to him. That's always bothered me."

"I'm so sorry."

"It's all right, hon." Lilly patted her hand again and put on a brighter smile. "I put all this behind me a long time ago. Sometimes, when you get to be my age, you get a little silly over memories."

"I didn't mean to—"

There was a tap on the door, and then it opened. "You home, Mom? You really ought to keep that door locked when you're here alone."

Lilly looked up and smiled as she dabbed her eyes with a tissue. "I'm not alone."

The man in the doorway was burly-looking and sixtyish, but his eyes under the heavy salt-and-pepper brows were large and dark, the image of his mother's.

"Carl." Lilly held out her hand, and he came to her. "Annie, Alice, this is Carl, my baby."

Her son smirked. "Yeah. I'm the baby." He gave her a piercing look. "You OK, Mom?"

"Oh, sure, hon. Just doing a little reminiscing. This is Annie, and this is Alice. Annie is Betsy Holden's grand-daughter. You remember Mrs. Holden, don't you?"

Carl nodded. "The cross-stitch lady? Yeah, I met her at Seaside a time or two a few years back. Nice lady." He offered Alice his hand. "Good to meet you both." He shook Annie's hand too. "Nice of you to come visit. Mom always enjoys company."

He looked at his mother again, searching her face.

"Don't be such a worrier," she scolded with a smile. "I'm not *that* fragile, you know."

Annie smiled at the man too. "I'm living in my grand-mother's house now. She was storing some old mementos for your mother, and I was just curious about them."

"I thought I put all your stuff in our basement after you sold the house." Carl grinned at Annie. "I think Mom kept every finger painting I ever did."

"Sounds like Annie with her grandkids," Alice said. "I can barely see her refrigerator for all the 'fine art.'"

Carl laughed and leaned against the wall, hands in his pockets. "Oh, don't get me started on my kids and grand-kids. Mom kept all their stuff too. At least everything she could get her hands on. My wife and daughter are just as bad. Must run in the family."

Lilly nodded serenely. "And I'll be a great-*great*-grand-mother anytime now."

"Oh, congratulations!" Annie clapped her hands together. "Congratulations to you both!"

"Yeah, we'll have another little rug rat in the family." Carl's voice was gruff, but there was more than a touch of pleasure in his eyes. "My little granddaughter Callie and that boy she married, they're expecting. Every time my phone rings, I think it must be the big call. It can't be too much longer now." He shook his head. "They're hardly more than babies themselves."

"Oh, hush, Carl," Lilly said. "Callie is twenty-one and out of college, and so is Max. When I was a girl, it wasn't so terribly unusual for a couple to get married right out of high school."

"Different times, Mom," Carl said. "Different times."

"I suppose during the war, everybody had to grow up fast." Annie glanced at Alice and stood up. "We ought to let the two of you visit now. We can talk some more later if you'd like to, Lilly."

Lilly beamed at her. "I'd like that very much. You come anytime, both of you. I'm free except for when I have physical therapy. Right now that's from two till three, Monday, Wednesday, and Friday. My shoulder's still not quite right, but just about."

"You try to do too much, Mom," Carl said.

"I'm not ready to hole up and quit," she told him firmly. "Not just yet."

"Like that'll ever happen," he said, rolling his eyes, and they both laughed.

"Anyway," she told Annie, "you come back when you have time to talk. And I'd love to see your pictures."

Annie drew her brows together. *My pictures?* She glanced to see Alice was equally puzzled, and then she realized Lilly must mean the pictures of Peter that Gram had kept for her. Why didn't she—

"Pictures, Mom?" Carl asked.

"Just some old family pictures Annie was telling me about. We won't bore Carl with our girl talk," Lilly said, patting her son's arm as she gave Annie a significant glance. "But you both come back anytime you want to. We'll talk again."

"Thank you," Annie said, standing and bringing Alice to her feet too. "It's been so nice to meet you both. We'll talk again, Lilly. And I'll bring those pictures for you to see."

"Thanks, hon."

Annie and Alice made their farewells and hurried back to the car.

Alice glanced back toward the apartment as they pulled away. "What was *that* all about?"

"I'm not really sure," Annie admitted. "Obviously, she didn't want her son to know what we were talking about."

"Wonder why."

Annie shrugged. "Sometimes older people are funny about things like that. I don't think she wants him to know she still has any of that stuff about Peter. She probably doesn't want him to think she's being disloyal to his father."

"Well, obviously, his father was the one she married, not Peter."

"True," Annie said, "but maybe only because Peter was dead."

"Still, he *is* dead, and so's her husband. I don't guess

she's hurting anything having some fond memories from when she was a girl."

Annie smiled. "You're right. She's certainly old enough to decide things like that for herself."

"Yeah. And at least you found out what you wanted to know. Lilly's here in Bremen and Peter's been gone for seventy years." Alice sighed. "So much for that little mystery."

"Oh, I don't know about that. There's still the question of exactly what happened to Peter. You heard Lilly. She never was told anything about how he died—what he was doing, not even where he was. She says she's over it, and I suppose she is, but it seemed to me that she still wants to know." Annie grinned at Alice and pulled out onto the highway. "And I'm going to find out."

~4~

Annie was a few minutes late to the meeting of the Hook and Needle Club that week. All of the ladies were already busy with their projects by the time she sat down with them.

"Sorry I'm late, girls." Annie pulled out the yarn for the light summer cardigan she was crocheting. "I was trying to find something and lost track of time."

"So what did you find out?" Peggy asked, looking up from her floral appliqué. "Anything on your young lovers?"

Everyone stopped work and looked expectantly at Annie.

"You won't believe it," Alice said as she marked her place on her cross-stitch pattern. "We found the girl. She's in one of those apartments in Bremen now, but she was living at Seaside for a while. One of the ladies there is her friend."

"She was?" Mary Beth shook her head. "I thought I knew everybody at Seaside by the time my mother passed away. Or maybe that was after Mom went."

"I think it was four or five years ago," Annie said.

"I don't think I ever met a Lilly there." Mary Beth thought for a moment as she rethreaded her needle. "Of course, Mom's last days are still a bit of a blur, so I can't swear I didn't."

"Her name's Lilly Bergstrom," Alice said, and Mary Beth smiled abruptly.

"OK, I do remember meeting a Mrs. Bergstrom a time or two in the hallway. Very nice-looking lady? Big brown eyes?"

"That's her," Annie said. "She was living at Seaside Hills after she hurt her shoulder and needed some help. Her son, Carl, lives in the area, but his wife's aunt already lives with his family, and Lilly didn't want to intrude. She seems pretty determined to keep her independence. But she still has friends over at Seaside who she visits now and then."

"She must be pretty old to have been a teenager in World War II," Peggy said, eyes wide. Stella's knitting needles were abruptly silent.

"I'll have you know, young lady," she said, lifting one silver eyebrow, "that I was around during that war too. We're not all dead yet."

Peggy's eyes widened even more, and then Stella smiled slyly and went back to her knitting. The rest of the ladies giggled.

"What about the boy?" Gwen asked. "Did you find out anything about him?"

Annie shook her head. "Just that he was killed the same year he enlisted. He was just eighteen."

"Did you find out what happened to him?" Kate asked softly.

Annie could only sigh. "Not really. I did some looking on the Internet. I found some Peter Lamberts who were obviously not the man I was looking for. Then I found a site that had some photocopies of the casualty lists by state. They had him listed there under 'Missing in Action or During Operational War Missions,' but the only information it showed was his name and rank, and his mother's name and address in Stony Point. It wasn't much help, I'm afraid."

"But that's not going to stop our Annie," Alice chimed in, and Annie laughed.

"No, it's not. I just wish I knew exactly where I should look for information. The Internet's great—except when it isn't."

"Have you tried contacting the War Department or the Army?" Mary Beth asked. "I guess they'd know."

"I haven't actually gotten that far." Annie started a new color on the striped cardigan she was crocheting for her grandson, John. "I'm not sure how much information they'd give out anyway. I'm not family or anything."

Mary Beth frowned, considering. "It's been what? Seventy years? Shouldn't that all be public information by now?"

"Maybe so." Annie paused as she studied her pattern once again. "I'll have to check it out."

For a few minutes, there was only the click of needles and the soft swish of fabric against fabric.

"Sooooo," Alice said, "where are we on planning the Easter banquet?"

"Well, that's partly why I was late," Annie admitted. "I was looking for those Easter table linens Gram had. I know they're around somewhere. Tell me what you all think of this: I was trying to figure out a good theme for the banquet ...."

"I thought it was Easter," Peggy said, her eyes twinkling.

"Well, yes," Annie said, "but what about Easter? I always remember Easter as going to church in the morning and then going over to my dad's mother's house for a family dinner. What if we set up the fellowship hall as if it were an old-fashioned family dining room? I mean, we'd still have to use our big tables and the folding chairs, but what if we had real tablecloths and napkins? Gram's Easter linens gave me the idea. We could use real china from all of our houses and real silverware and that sort of thing."

"We could mix it all up and give it a 'collected over the generations' kind of look," Mary Beth said, nodding. "Maybe we could even get a few antiques—some oil lamps and other knickknacks, that kind of thing—to put on the tables. What do you think?"

"I like it," Alice said, "though it might be a challenge to make sure everybody gets back what she brings."

"We could keep a list of who brought how many of what," Kate suggested. "That ought to take care of it."

"That seems fair enough." Gwen paused, searching for a particular ball of yarn in her bag. "Keep in mind, though, that there's always something that gets broken in big banquets like this one. I don't know if it's a good idea for us to bring our very best china."

"No, probably not," Annie said. "Just bring a good variety of old-fashioned dishes. And, whatever you do, don't bring something you couldn't bear to lose. I'm sure everybody will be as careful as possible, but as Gwen said, accidents happen." She smiled at the circle of friends. "Now that's just one idea. We can certainly do something else if someone has another idea."

"I like it," Stella said, her knitting needles clicking. "It'll be a nice change from the same old disposable plates and plastic forks that break off in your food. It'll mean more work for all of us, of course, but it *is* a special occasion."

"So what do you think?" Alice asked. "Are we good with this, or should we talk it over a little more? Any other ideas?"

Kate shook her head. "I like it."

"Me too," Peggy said.

"All right then ..." Mary Beth waited an expectant moment and then smiled. "If we're all agreed, let's do it."

*   *   *   *

Once the meeting was over, Annie headed back to her car where she saw a familiar car parked in front of Town Hall. Ian Butler, the mayor of Stony Point and Annie's more-than-just-a-friend, was obviously in, so she decided to drop by. Mrs. Nash, Ian's secretary, was on the telephone when Annie came in, but she smiled and waved her through to his office.

Ian was also on the phone, but his brown eyes warmed when he saw Annie, and he leapt up to pull a chair over to the front of his desk as he continued his conversation.

"No, Mrs. Adams, I'm sorry, but I can't do anything about the rats in your garage. It's not really part of what local government does. Have you called an exterminator?" He settled Annie into the chair with a wink. "No, ma'am, that's not something Animal Control is responsible for either. Stray dogs are more in their line. Or wild animals." He nodded. "Yes, I understand the rats are wild, but—"

Annie had to cover her mouth to keep from laughing aloud. Poor Ian. He was always expected to fix everything for everybody in Stony Point. And bless him if he didn't try to do it too.

"No, ma'am, I can't recommend one in particular, but I'm sure you can find a good one in your phone book or on the Internet." Again he nodded. "Right. Just look under exterminators or pest control." He paused, giving Annie a good-naturedly exasperated look. "I'm sure they do charge for their services, Mrs. Adams, but that's what keeps them in business and able to come help you when you need them." He nodded once more. "All right then. You give them a call. Yes, I'm sure they can. Have a good afternoon. Yes, OK, I'll—all right. Goodbye now."

He hung up. Eyes twinkling, Annie smiled sympathetically.

"I take it Mrs. Adams has rats now."

He grinned. "At least she didn't call Wally Carson this time. He *tried* to get those squirrels out of her attic for her, but as he told her, he's a handyman not a wild-animal trainer."

Annie laughed. "I have just about everything in the world up in my attic, you know, but not squirrels, thank goodness. Not squirrels."

"Not even a skunk or two?"

"No, I'm happy to report, but I *did* come across something pretty interesting when I was looking for some things for the Easter banquet."

"Oh, right," Ian tapped his chin with one finger. "That *is* coming up, isn't it?"

"Funny how they schedule these Easter banquets right around Easter every year."

Ian reached across the desk for her hand. "What do you think about going with me?"

"I guess you'll never know unless you ask me." She gave

him a coy little smile, lacing her fingers through his, and he gave them a squeeze. Then he cleared his throat.

"Will you, Annie Dawson, accompany me, Ian Butler, prestigious mayor of beautiful Stony Point, Maine, to the upcoming Easter banquet which—as I understand it—will take place on Easter Sunday, to be followed by a not-to-be-equaled egg hunt, weather permitting?"

She sat up very straight in her chair and solemnly raised her right hand. "I, Annie Dawson, would be quite pleased— and even delighted—to accompany said prestigious mayor to said banquet and egg hunt, if said mayor doesn't mind me having some kitchen duties to see to from time to time."

"So be it." He seized the ceremonial gavel on the corner of his desk and brought it down sharply. Then he grinned. "Now you're stuck with me."

Annie laughed. "OK, since I'm stuck with you, you might as well make yourself useful."

"Your wish is my command, my lady, as long as it doesn't involve pest control."

"Nothing like that. Just another of my unanswered questions."

"Something up in your attic? A left-handed monkey wrench? The Hope Diamond? Stanley Livingston?"

Annie tried to look stern. "Nothing like that."

"What did you find this time?" He chuckled. "I swear, a man could never get bored with you around."

She pursed her lips, suppressing a smile. "Be nice, or for Christmas I'm giving you that stuffed caiman I found up there a couple of weeks ago."

"A caiman?"

"Yes. You know—a kind of alligator from South or Central America. Fortunately, the stuffed one in Gram's attic is a small one."

Ian laughed. "I know what they are. I just ... a real one?" He shook his head. "Your grandmother had some interesting friends, that's for sure."

"Tell me about it. But, no, I'll spare you the caiman ..." She pretended to give him a stern glance. "... this time."

He shook his head, still chuckling. "No, really, what did you find?"

"Just some stuff from the Second World War. Some letters, a diary, and some pictures." She grinned. "And an old 78-rpm record of *Don't Sit Under the Apple Tree*."

"Ah, the good old Andrews Sisters. With music like that, no way we could have lost the war." Ian shook his head. "Now *that* was an interesting time in history. It's amazing how just about everybody in the whole country pulled together to support the war effort."

"Really. And it was amazing how much people sacrificed back then. We don't know how good we have it now. I wonder how many are left who served in the armed forces back then?"

"They'd be pretty well up there in age," Ian said. "Even the young ones would be pushing ninety by now."

"Oh, and some of them were so terribly young. The diary I found belonged to a teenage girl whose boyfriend was sent overseas at age eighteen. And I know some of the boys were even younger."

"I'm afraid so." Ian shook his head. "Anyway, your teenager and her boyfriend are probably both gone by now."

"No, actually. I talked to the girl—I should say, woman. She had been over at Seaside Hills, and Gram was keeping some of her things that she didn't have room for there. She's living in an apartment in Bremen now."

"Wow. She must have some great stories to tell. Did her beau come back and marry her?"

Annie gave him a sad smile. "I'm afraid not. He was killed the same year he enlisted."

"That's tough," Ian said. "What happened?"

"That's what I've been asking myself. Lilly—the lady who left her diary with Gram—says the Army didn't tell his mother much of anything, just that he was believed killed in action. There was no body. Nothing. Poor thing, she never really knew when or where he died or what he was doing. I'm sure she'd still like to know."

Ian grinned. "You mean *you'd* like to know."

"Little ol' me?" She batted her lashes at him and put on her very best Texas drawl. "Ah jest don't know what y'all mean."

"Uh-huh."

"OK, OK. So I do want to know. She says Peter—that's the boy—spoke fluent German and wanted to be a spy, but she doesn't know if that's what he was doing when he was killed or not."

"A spy, eh? Every boy's dream job."

"Yeah." Annie propped her chin on her hand. "How do you suppose I could find out more about what he was involved in?"

Ian laughed. "What'd you say he was? Eighteen? I doubt that he ever got the chance to be involved in espionage."

"I don't know. You should see the pictures of this boy. He looked German. His parents were German. He might have been perfect for undercover work."

Ian considered that for a moment. "I don't know if the OSS would have kept a lot of records of undercover missions back then."

"The OSS?"

"Office of Strategic Services. They were set up during the war to handle all the intelligence and covert operations—the CIA of their day. Anyway, I think they would have been extra careful about leaks with anything related to spying. Have you checked with the War Department for this guy's service records? I don't know. Maybe some of the veterans' organizations could help you. Or maybe just an Internet search could point you in the right direction. I'm always amazed at the variety of information out there."

"I did do a quick search," Annie said. "I found a rose expert and a juggler and a basketball player, but none of them was this Peter Lambert. I found a site with scans of casualty lists and found him there, but there was only his name, rank, and address listed. No details about how he died. I haven't done much of anything else yet, but if I were Lilly, I would want to know. Even now. Wouldn't you?"

Ian shrugged. "I don't know. Probably. But I think after this long you'd have to let it go. No matter how much she loved him, she'd have to forget about him and move on."

"Yes, I suppose that's true. And that's what she did too. She eventually married and had a family. She's about to have her first great-*great*-grandchild."

"I guess that counts as moving on." Ian chuckled, and then his expression turned wistful. "It's something we all have to do. We couldn't make it in life if we didn't."

"But not forget," Annie said. "Even when we move on, that doesn't mean we have to forget."

"No. I shouldn't have said forget. We shouldn't try to forget, not the good things. We just can't let the memories keep us from living now." He winked and squeezed her hand. "Speaking of now, it's about half past lunch. Would you care to join me at the Fish House?"

"That would be great," Annie said. "Then you can tell me all about how to track down the information I'm looking for."

"Well, let me see." Ian's brow furrowed. "You might try the War Department or even the VFW. You could go over to the Community Center when they meet on Monday and see if someone there can help you."

"OK. Don't you have some big political favors you could call in?"

That made Ian laugh. "My political clout and a few bucks will buy you lunch. That's all I can guarantee." He stood up and offered her his hand. "Will that do for the moment?"

"It would be divine."

~ 5 ~

The Grand Avenue Fish House was strategically placed to offer the finest view of Stony Point's harbor. Of course, it was even more beautiful at night with the stars twinkling above and reflected in the dark water of the ocean, but even on a grayish day when the weather couldn't seem to make up its mind, the view was lovely. The wind was blowing up little whitecaps here and there, but the day was clear enough for Annie to see Butler's Lighthouse standing watch on the harbor.

"It must be nice," she said as she looked out over the water, and Ian smiled.

"What must be nice?"

"Having your own lighthouse."

Ian chuckled. "It's not actually mine, you know."

"Well, it's named for your family, isn't it?"

He nodded.

"It just sort of makes you part of this place," she said. "It's nice."

He didn't say anything for a while, as though he were trying to decide whether or not to speak at all.

"You don't have to have generations of family history to be a part of a place," he said at last, reaching across the table to take her hand. "You're definitely a part of Stony Point—a very important part. In fact—"

"Good afternoon. My name is Derek, and I'll be taking excellent care of you today." The young man smiled professionally. "May I start you off with something to drink?"

Ian chuckled softly and released her hand. "What would you like, Annie?"

"Coffee, please," Annie told the waiter, and Ian nodded. "Make that two."

"Two coffees," Derek said, and he set an open menu in front of each of them. "Our special today is our lobster lasagna, which is tender, steamed Maine lobster chunks in between layers of pasta with our special Alfredo sauce, fresh spinach, and ricotta, cheddar, and parmesan cheeses. It's served with a tossed garden salad and oven-toasted garlic bread. We're also featuring our New England crab cakes with a seafood pasta salad and boiled potatoes or freshly steamed vegetables. Our selection of fresh fish is on the back of the menu, and I highly recommend the grilled haddock." He smiled. "I'll give you a chance to look over the menu and be back in just a minute with your coffee."

The waiter disappeared as quickly as he had appeared.

"What sounds good?" Ian asked once he had spent a few minutes scanning his menu.

"I think the haddock sounds wonderful. I'm tempted by the crab cakes, but I think I'll have the haddock and steamed broccoli if they have it. How about you?"

"Shrimp casserole and clam chowder for me."

She beamed at him. "Yummy. I do love the food here. Not that I don't miss our Southern barbecue or Tex-Mex once in a while, but I can never argue with New England clam chowder."

"That's because you belong here." Again he reached over to take her hand. "As I said, you're a very important part of Stony Point, and you're very important to—"

"Have we decided?"

The waiter set down their coffees along with a small pitcher of fresh cream, and Ian again released Annie's hand.

"I think so," he said, just the tiniest bit of tightness in his voice. "Grilled haddock and steamed broccoli for the lady, and I'll have the shrimp casserole and clam chowder."

The waiter nodded. "Excellent choice, sir. And on your salads?"

"The house dressing, please," Annie said.

Ian handed the waiter their menus. "The same for me."

"Thank you, sir. I'll have those salads right out."

"He knows just when to interrupt," Ian said when the waiter had disappeared again.

Annie giggled. "I think waiters have some mysterious radar that lets them know exactly when you don't want them coming by."

Ian grinned and then his face turned more serious. "All I was going to say is that you're an important part of Stony Point, and you're important to me."

She looked down. She had known for some time that Ian had feelings for her. Serious feelings. Up until now, they had managed a comfortable friendship, and she didn't want to lose that. She and Ian had attended social functions together and had gone on a few dates—they had even shared a few tender kisses. Ian was such a gentleman, and he hadn't pressed the matter. Annie had taken the "we're just friends" tack, but she knew in her heart that Ian Butler was more than just a friend.

She had loved Wayne from the moment they met, and losing him had been the hardest thing she had ever gone through. But the pain had passed. She hadn't forgotten, but she had healed. Lilly's sweetheart, Peter, had wanted her to go on with her life if he didn't come home, and Annie knew without a doubt that Wayne would have felt the same way.

Still, she couldn't help feeling a little—she didn't know the exact word to best describe it—disloyal, perhaps, for thinking about dating seriously again. Annie thought about the times she and Ian had gone out. But those didn't really count as dates, did they? What about this one?

Ian had taken hold of her hand again, and he was looking at her with those earnest brown eyes. He was awfully attractive. She had never been able to deny that. And he was a wonderful man too—honest and kind and trustworthy. Gallant even. How many men were there like that anymore? But still ....

"Hello! Anybody in there?" Annie blinked, and Ian chuckled. "You were a million miles away, Annie. Want some company?"

She blushed faintly. "Sorry about that. I was just thinking."

"About?"

"About ... things." She took a sip of her coffee, keeping her eyes on the cup. "About what you were saying."

"I didn't really even get started yet, you know."

"I know." She glanced up at him and then back at her coffee cup. "But I think I know where you were going."

He winced. "That obvious, is it?"

"No. Not really. It's just, after this long, it's sort of a logical next step. You have every right to wonder where we go from here."

"I'm not trying to put any pressure on you, Annie." Once more he took her hand. "I just want you to know how special you are to me. After Arianna died, I never thought I'd ever be interested in anyone else. Then you showed up in Stony Point, and I knew right away you were different." He grinned a little. "Maybe what I liked best was that you just wanted to be friends. And that's all I wanted too ..." His face colored a little. "... at first."

"Ian, I—"

"No, let me finish. As I said, you're really special to me, and I—"

"Two salads with house dressing." The waiter set two bowls of leafy green salad in front of them along with a basket of bread. Then he held up a pepper grinder. "Would you care for fresh pepper on yours, ma'am?"

Anne smiled and looked up. "Yes, please."

"And you, sir?"

"Yes," Ian said, managing a smile too. "Thank you very much."

The waiter gave both salads a light sprinkling of pepper. "Your entrees are almost ready. I'll have them out for you in just a few minutes."

Ian laughed once he was gone again. "You know, I hadn't really planned on having this conversation today anyway. It just sort of ... came out. Maybe we should just forget all about it for now and enjoy our lunch. What do you say?"

She patted his hand and then released it. "I think that's a good idea."

They both started on their salads, and for a moment the only sound was the crunch of lettuce and croutons. Annie scrambled for something innocuous to talk about.

"I was pretty surprised when I found Lilly Bergstrom so near to Stony Point after all these years."

Smiling, Ian swallowed and touched his napkin to his mouth. "I bet you were. How is she, by the way? I mean, is she doing all right? She's got to be what? Eighty-six? Eighty-seven?"

"I didn't ask her, but she was seventeen in 1943, so you do the math. And, yes, she seems to be in really good shape. Still trim and really quite nice looking. You wouldn't think she was older than seventy or so."

Ian nodded. "Amazing how some people age so well, and others have a really hard time of it. That reminds me. I talked to my aunt the other day."

"How's she doing?"

"Oh, pretty well, considering. Taking care of someone with Alzheimer's is a pretty tough job."

Annie gave him an understanding smile. "How is your uncle?"

"He's about the same, I'm afraid. My aunt says he still has a few good days, but mostly he doesn't know her or anybody."

Annie shook her head. "I'm sorry. He's not even all that old, is he?"

"He's seventy-eight." Ian's dark eyes were somber. "It's a shame too, because physically, he's doing well. It would be nice if everybody could be like your Mrs. Bergstrom, you know?"

"It's funny," Annie said. "Everybody seems surprised that, at her age, she's not either dead or bedridden. I think there are a lot of older people who are doing just fine, thank you very much. I had a great-uncle who passed away a couple of years ago when he was ninety-four. He needed a little help by then, but he was still as sharp as a tack. Another great-uncle of mine just turned eighty-eight. He's the one that amazes me." Annie grinned. "He lives at home by himself. He still drives, and he still does a little work now and then for his old boss. He does his own laundry and microwaves a mean frozen dinner."

Ian laughed. "Your family must have some pretty good genes."

"I like to think so. Of course, that's all on my father's side. I guess I'll have to wait and see what genes I end up with."

"Yeah, I guess none of us know till we get there," Ian said. "It's best to make the most of the present since we never know what time we have left, huh?"

"I'll certainly drink to that." Annie lifted her coffee cup to him in a toast, and he raised his cup in response, dark eyes warm.

"And to good company!"

She smiled back at him. He *was* nice to have around. *Awfully* nice.

*   *   *   *

Later that week, Annie got to work gathering up things she wanted to loan out for the Easter banquet. Boots—the gray cat that Annie inherited from Betsy along with Grey Gables—always liked to get into mischief, so Annie was careful to make sure the cat didn't follow her up the stairs into the attic. Annie needed no distractions this time; she still hadn't found the Easter linens she was looking for, but she knew there were at least two boxes of vintage dishes up there. They weren't collector's items or anything, just good, old-fashioned dinnerware that would look nice and homey on the banquet tables. If she could only figure out where she had last seen them.

She found a stack of dessert plates with a pretty rose pattern at the bottom of a box of Christmas ornaments. Once she had shifted the ornaments into a smaller box, she could use the box with the plates to collect whatever else she could find that would work for the banquet. Seven dinner plates with rustic scenes on them as well as a matching serving platter were stacked on the shelf near where she had found the box of Lilly's memorabilia. She put the dishes in the box with the other plates and then looked again at the collection of letters.

She didn't quite know why it interested her so much. She really needed to concentrate on preparing for the Easter banquet, but she couldn't help wondering about what exactly had happened to Peter. And maybe more important now, about letting Lilly know whatever she found out.

Impulsively, she pulled one of the letters out of the stack and opened it. It was dated July 29, 1943.

Dearest Lilly,

I'll be getting out of boot camp before long. Then I guess I'll be shipped out somewhere. They haven't really told me what I'll be doing, but I told them about my background. I think they can use me. It's a little scary to think about it too much, since you know what happens if you get caught behind enemy lines out of uniform. But I can't help think I was meant to do this sort of thing.

Of course, most of the older guys just laugh at me and tell me I'm green as grass. My sergeant told me not to make any big plans about knocking off Hitler or anything just yet. He's a card. But I suppose they're right. That doesn't mean I won't want to do my part to end this war as quick as possible.

I haven't forgotten your birthday is coming up, honey. You'll be eighteen and all grown up. I hope you like the present I have for you and don't want to send it back. At least not for a long, long time.

Miss you something awful.

> *Love always,*
> *Peter*

With a smile, Annie put the letter back into the faded envelope. Lilly had mentioned him coming home on leave after boot camp. She'd have to ask her what Peter had brought for her birthday. Probably not much in those days, but it seemed pretty likely that she would have treasured it. She had certainly treasured the bits and pieces that were left of him.

Annie pulled Lilly's box off the shelf and put it on the floor next to her box of dishes. Maybe she'd just give Lilly a call in a little while. Lilly had already said she'd like to see those photos again. The letters and other things too, no doubt. Annie traced one finger over the faded label on the old record and grinned. Maybe Lilly had a turntable.

~ 6 ~

Once Annie had gathered up all the old dishes she could find and had packed them into the dishwasher, she gave Lilly a call. Lilly said she was free anytime after one o'clock, and Annie told her she'd come by then. So, it was a little after one when Annie knocked on Lilly's door.

"Come in."

Annie opened the door and was surprised to find that Lilly wasn't there. Another woman, stooped and wizened, was sitting in a wheelchair on the other side of the room. Annie remembered her from Seaside Hills and smiled.

"Hello. I came to see Lilly. You're Mrs. Madison, right?"

The other woman smiled in return. "Call me Nita, and you're Annie. I remember you from Seaside. My granddaughter dropped me off for a visit while she gets her hair done, and then she and I are going to have a late lunch. Just us two. Please, come in and sit down."

Annie did.

"Lilly said it was OK if I came by. Will she be back soon?"

"Oh, yes. She just went to get a sweater for me to borrow. Are you the Annie who's finding out about Peter?"

Annie nodded. "Would you like to see a picture of him?"

Nita grinned. "Lilly tells me he was really worth looking at."

Annie rummaged in the box she was carrying and brought out the picture of Peter standing on the porch in his then-new uniform. "What do you think?"

"Oooh." Nita's eyes twinkled. "Definitely worth looking at. Oh, to be twenty again."

"You know you wouldn't want to be twenty again, Nita." Lilly came into the room, handed Nita a knitted red sweater, and sat down on the couch. "I wouldn't want to go back to being that age for anything. I've finally figured out who and what I am, and I don't want to have to go through the process all over again, thank you very much."

Annie chuckled. "Hi, Lilly. How are you today?"

"Oh, fine. You know, more and more, I'm thinking I'm about through with physical therapy. They're wonderful to me at the facility, of course, but my shoulder is finally getting back to normal again, and I can do most everything for myself now. It seems a little silly to keep going when I really feel fine."

"But you always come visit us at Seaside after your therapy," Nita said, sinking a little in her wheelchair. "We'd miss you."

Lilly reached over and took her hand. "I could still come visit. I'd still have lots of time for that."

"I'm glad you're doing better," Annie said. "And all this might make you feel even better still."

Lilly's eyes lit up as Annie placed the box of keepsakes on her lap.

"Oh, I've been wanting to see this ever since you first came by." She started pulling out the pictures and letters. "Here I'd thought this was gone all this time. I tried not to let it bother me, but I suppose it did, deep down. You're a sweetheart to bring it back to me."

"I'm so glad I found it," Annie said. "I'm so glad I found *you*."

There was a knock at the door, and then it opened.

"I'm back." A young woman came into the room, her hair freshly cut and highlighted. "What do you think?"

"You look beautiful as always, Caroline," Lilly said, and Caroline smiled.

"Thanks, Mrs. Bergstrom. Are you ready to go have lunch, Grandma?"

"Of course!" Nita beamed at her. "We'll be going, Lilly. Thanks for letting me borrow a sweater. You two have fun."

She handed the picture of Peter back to Lilly and waved as she was rolled away. Lilly waved back and then looked fondly at the photograph.

"I remember that day like it was this morning. He had just gotten his first leave after boot camp. He was laughing at me because my father had just given me that camera for my birthday, and I didn't have a clue how to use it. I hate to admit how much of that first roll of film was wasted. And the second. It's not like the cameras we have now where you can just snap away and erase anything you don't want."

Annie giggled. "Sounds like you both had fun anyway."

"Oh, we did." She looked at the picture again, a wistful, faraway look in her eyes, and then she looked back into the box and took out one of the very small letters. "Now here's something you don't see anymore. Have you ever heard of V-mail?"

Annie grinned, taking the pint-sized envelope from her. "I've heard of it, but I've never seen it."

The way I understand it, the original letters were copied to film, shipped back to the U.S., and then printed in tiny versions and mailed to the individual addresses. It saved on the bulk and weight of the thousands of letters servicemen sent back home every day." Lilly took the letter from inside the envelope and squinted, holding it a little farther away from her. "I imagine the small print was hard for some parents and grandparents to make out, but I guess they didn't mind too much as long as they heard from their boys."

She passed the V-mail letter to Annie. It wasn't actually a letter. It was a Christmas card. It showed a cartoon of an American eagle flying away with a protesting Hitler in one claw and a pouting Mussolini in the other. The printed caption read, "This—and a Merry Christmas for you!" Under the picture was handwritten, "You can see we have them well in hand. Lots of love, Peter."

They both chuckled, and Lilly put it back into its envelope and then brought out the record.

"And this song—it was almost a joke between us. He'd always warn me about sitting under the apple tree, and I'd tell him to watch where he sat himself. I don't think it was in him to ever stray though. He just wasn't that way."

Annie gave her an understanding smile. "Sounds like he loved you a lot."

"I think so," Lilly said softly, and she took out the little silver ring with the lover's knot and slid it onto her finger. It still fit. "I know I loved him."

"I hope you don't mind, but I read another of his letters earlier when I was packing up this box for you. He was talking about something he got you for your birthday, something he hoped you wouldn't want to send back. I was wondering if maybe it was that ring."

Lilly stroked her finger over the tarnished silver. "No. He gave me this before he went away—just a reminder of his promises to me. And I never took it off. Not until I agreed to marry Jimmy."

"But what did he get you for your birthday?"

*   *   *   *

July, 1943

Lilly smiled as her father scooted his chair up to the table and eyed the food her mother had set out.

"You ought to have birthdays more often, honey. I don't think I've seen a meal like this since before the war started."

It really wasn't a fancy meal. Lilly's mother and two of the neighbor ladies had pooled their ration coupons and bought a nice roast and all the fixings with it. Now all three families were gathered for Lilly's birthday dinner: Lilly and her parents, Mr. and Mrs. Dubois and their little boy Mike, and Mrs. Bergstrom and her two girls. None of them had really had a special meal since Jimmy Bergstrom had shipped out the previous year.

Lilly still wasn't quite sure why they should do this for her birthday. She wasn't used to the fuss. But it was fun anyway, and it was nice to have their neighbors over for the celebration.

Lilly's mom had just set the roast on the table when the doorbell rang. Shaking her head, she took off her oven mitts. "I can't imagine who that might be."

With a wink at Mrs. Bergstrom, she went through to the living room. Lilly heard the front door open and then her mother's voice.

"Come in. You're just in time for dinner."

"Evening, folks."

Lilly turned to see Jimmy Bergstrom standing in the dining room door in uniform, hat in hand and grinning at his mother who was already standing up with her arms outstretched.

"Jimmy!"

He caught her up in a big hug, and then his little sisters were tugging at him and hugging him too, and everyone was talking at once.

"Good to have you home, Jimmy," Lilly's father said at last, and he pulled out the chair next to Lilly. "Have a seat."

"Thank you, sir." Jimmy sat down, glancing at Lilly as he scooted up to the table. "Hello, Lilly. Happy birthday."

She gave him a friendly smile. "Thanks. I thought this was kind of a big celebration just for me. Now I see it's for you too. Welcome home."

"We thought it would be fun to make one big party out of it when we found out when Jimmy would be home," his mother said. "It was his idea to surprise you."

He gave her a sheepish little grin, and Lilly passed him the potatoes. "It's wonderful to have him here," she told his mother brightly. "It's almost like having a real brother."

She could see the disappointment in Jimmy's eyes at that, but she didn't want him or his mother to get the wrong idea. Oh, why couldn't it have been Peter at the door instead of Jimmy?

But it was a lovely meal, a special treat, and afterward, when there was hardly a scrap left, her mother got up from the table.

"That was delicious," Mr. Dubois said. "All you ladies did a fine job."

There was a general murmur around the table echoing this sentiment, and Mom glowed under the praise.

"But that's not all." She got up from the table and nodded at the Dubois boy. "OK, Mike. Whenever you're ready."

With a devilish grin on his freckled face, Mike jumped up and switched off the lights. A few seconds later, the table was lit with the soft glow of candles as Mrs. Pryce brought in Lilly's birthday cake.

"How in the world did you get enough ration coupons for sugar and chocolate for that?" Lilly asked over the oohing and ahing of the others.

"A little creative bartering," her mother said, a twinkle in her eyes. "OK, everybody."

They all joined in singing happy birthday wishes, clapping and cheering afterwards.

"Come on, Lilly," Mrs. Dubois said. "Close your eyes and make a wish."

Lilly stood up, squeezing her eyes shut tightly, but she wasn't going to make a wish. No use wasting it on something she couldn't have. Oh, if only ....

She wished anyway and blew out the candles. But before she could open them, someone's hands were over her eyes. There was giggling and whispering all around her, and then, all together, everyone said, "Guess who!"

She smiled good-naturedly. "Ummm, President Roosevelt?"

But then she put her hands over the hands that covered her eyes. They were a man's hands, she could tell. A young man's. She knew those hands.

She pulled them away from her face and turned, the tears already springing to her eyes. "Peter!" She threw herself into his arms, laughing and crying all at once, to see him there, strong and handsome in his uniform. And he was real. "Peter, Peter."

He only held her close, and she could tell by the little catch in his breathing that he didn't dare try to say anything.

"Surprised, honey?" her father asked.

She nodded and found she couldn't say much of anything either, but everyone was looking at her, waiting for her to speak. Everyone, that is, except Jimmy who was staring down at his empty plate.

"I'm sorry you missed supper," she said finally, and everybody laughed.

"I had dinner with my mother," Peter said as he sat down beside her. "But I sure didn't want to miss this great cake."

"Where were you hiding anyway?" she asked him, giving her mother a suspicious glance.

"All right, all right," Mom admitted. "He's been out in the kitchen for the last ten minutes, waiting for me to come get the cake."

"I almost busted in here ahead of time," Peter admitted. "I couldn't stand the wait." He squeezed her hand, looking a little apologetic. "I'm afraid I don't have anything for you but me. Just getting here took nearly all the dough I had. But I thought—"

She snuggled close to him. "You're exactly what I wanted. And I won't be sending you back until they make me."

7

*L*illy smiled shyly at Annie, and her cheeks turned pink. "Peter got to stay for three days. That was his wonderful present to me. We spent most of that time, morning till night, together. I think his mother was a little jealous, but he spent the evenings at home with her. The three of us even had dinner together a couple of times. Looking back, I still wish we'd gone ahead and gotten married when we could. I know we were young. It probably would have been a foolish thing to do. But still ...."

She laughed then and slipped the ring off again.

"Don't misunderstand me, Annie. I loved my husband. Jimmy was a good man, and he was always good to me." Her eyes twinkled. "If Peter was built like Errol Flynn, I guess Jimmy was more like Wallace Beery. But he had a heart of gold and was just as sweet as anything to me. Still, it was hard sometimes. I guess real life, learning to live with another person—a real person and not just a memory—is hard. But he took care of me, and I know he loved me. I'm glad he was there when Peter couldn't be."

Annie nodded. She sometimes wondered if her memories of Wayne were becoming a little blurred. As much as she had adored him, as much as she had appreciated him as a husband and as a man, there had always been things to work through, to compromise on, to make up for. That was just the nature of marriage. As Lilly had said, learning to live with another person, a real person and not just a memory, was hard. Lilly realized, at least to some degree, that she had idealized the Peter of her memories. Maybe Annie had done the same with her own lost love. Poor Ian. He didn't stand a chance against a memory. At least he didn't stand a chance if she wouldn't let him.

Lilly put the ring back into the box.

"After the war was over, Jimmy came home on leave. He had already reenlisted. He wanted to be a career soldier, and he asked me to marry him." She smiled a little sheepishly. "I couldn't even consider it. Not then. I knew Peter was gone, but I just couldn't. Jimmy asked if he could at least write to me, and I said he could. He did too—at least once a week. Sometimes two or three times. He was good about that. A few years later, after he had been stationed in Berlin, he came home again. By then, I had finished college. I had a job doing secretarial work for one of my dad's lawyer friends, but I wasn't sure what I really wanted to do."

*　　*　　*　　*

June 1950

Lilly pinned the other end of the sheet to the clothesline and wiped a trickle of sweat from her forehead. Then she stretched a kink out of her back. There were three more sheets and a bedspread left in the basket, but the summer sun would have them all dry in no time. She was just stretching up to hang another sheet when she heard the back gate squeak open.

"Lilly?"

She turned, blushing, and tucked her hair under the kerchief she had tied around her head. "Jimmy! I thought you were still in Berlin."

Jimmy Bergstrom smiled at her, his brown hair freshly cut, his corporal's uniform starched and pressed, and a dozen red roses in his hand. "I'm about to get shipped out to Italy, but I got a nice long furlough so I could come back home first."

She wiped her hand on her apron and took the one he offered. "And you came to see me?"

"Who else would I want to see?"

She smiled. He was terribly sweet.

"Help me get the rest of this up, and we'll go inside where it's cooler."

He propped the bouquet against the laundry basket, and between them, they made quick work of the sheets and the bedspread. Then Jimmy picked up the roses again.

"I—I thought you might like these."

Lilly was pleased; it was very thoughtful of him.

"They're beautiful. Thank you." She took the flowers and gave him the empty laundry basket in exchange. "I made some lemonade. Would you like some?"

They sat on the couch drinking well-iced lemonade and eating fresh oatmeal cookies while he told her his plans.

"You're going to Italy?" she asked, and he nodded.

"Yeah."

"Oh, that's wonderful. I always wanted to see the world, especially Italy and France and Spain. Germany too, though I guess it's still fairly torn up right now."

Something flickered in his eyes. "I hope they don't send me back to Germany ever again. I've been stuck there since the end of the war."

She took a sip of lemonade, smiling at him. "But it looks like such a pretty place."

"Oh, it is—like out of a storybook. But there's a lot more of the world I'd like to see." He took a deep breath. "And I'd like you to see it with me."

She glanced over at the bouquet that was now in the vase on the coffee table. Red roses. Passionate love. She shouldn't have been surprised. Truly, she wasn't. This had been coming for some time now.

"Jimmy—"

"Don't turn me down, Lil. Please."

"But I could never—"

"I know. I know. You still love Peter."

"It's not that." Well, yes, it *was* that. Or maybe it was that she had never met anyone who could take Peter's place. "I'm just—I'm happy as I am. I don't think I'm ready to marry anyone. I might never be."

"But, Lilly—" He took her hand, his dark eyes pleading. "Peter wouldn't have wanted you to be alone your whole life. He wasn't a dog-in-the-manger kind of guy."

Keep me in a special place in your heart, and someday, fall in love with someone else. Promise me you will, Lilly.

Tears sprang to her eyes. "No. No, he wasn't. It just—"

She squeezed the hand that held hers, and he stood up, shoving his hands in his pockets as he paced.

"It's been almost seven years, Lil. If he was

coming back, if he was somehow still alive, and he really wanted to come back, don't you think he would have by now?"

She nodded, blinking the tears away. "I know he's dead. I know he's not coming back. It just wouldn't be fair to you, Jimmy. I love you. I promise, I love you very much. But not the way I loved him. Not the way I love him still. Not the way you deserve your wife to love you."

He looked down at his freshly polished shoes and said nothing.

"Come on." She patted the couch cushion beside her. "Finish your lemonade and have another cookie."

He sat down, and she took his hand again.

"Besides," she said softly, smiling a little. "You're an Army man now. You could be sent anywhere in the world. My parents are getting on now. Mom isn't in the best health. I need to be here for them. There isn't any other family to look after them."

"They're not going to be around forever you know," Jimmy said. "Then you'll be all by yourself."

"Besides, I love this house. I love Stony Point. Everything I love is right here."

He shrugged. "I don't have to be in the Army. If you—"

"And what would you do to make a living?" She turned her head to one side, lips pursed. "You've never done anything else."

"I'd figure out something. I promise I'd take care of you. I promise."

"And how many times have you told me how much you love being in the Army?" She made her expression as gentle and understanding as she could. "No use us both being miserable."

He flinched as if that had hurt him, and then he managed a bit of a smile and stood up.

"I guess that's that then." He slipped his hand out of hers. "I won't bug you about it any more. Thanks for being straight with me anyhow."

"I'm so sorry."

"May I—" He looked up at the ceiling, blinking hard. "May I still write to you?"

"I hope you will." She smiled up at him. "I do love you, Jimmy."

"I love you too, Lil." He smoothed his hair and put on his hat. "Maybe not enough."

Her forehead wrinkled. "What do you mean?"

He only shook his head. "I'd do anything for you, Lil, right or wrong. I guess if I loved you more, I'd just let you go, but I can't seem to do it." He smiled faintly and leaned down to kiss her cheek. "Write to me."

*   *   *   *

"So you turned him down again," Annie said softly.

"Yes. It was true, though. I was happy just the way I was. It wasn't a very exciting life, I suppose, but I liked it. I always loved Stony Point, and getting Jimmy's letters from Italy was always a special event."

"You didn't wish just a little bit that you could go traveling too?"

There was a tiny gleam in Lilly's eyes. "Well, maybe a

little. OK, if I was going to be honest with myself, a whole lot. But I wasn't lying to him when I said my parents needed me. My father was working hard, trying to save up enough to eventually retire. Mom had some heart problems and needed someone with her most of the time. It's not like today when doctors can fix just about anything."

Annie shook her head. "I guess you've seen some big changes in your life."

"Amazing, isn't it? Wouldn't I have loved to have a microwave and cellphone back then? And I think our soldiers would have liked to have something to eat besides Spam and powdered eggs."

"I had a great-uncle in the Navy during the war, and he wouldn't even look at Spam afterward." Annie shuddered, grinning. "I don't mind Spam so much, but I can't imagine those powdered eggs."

"I never saw them, much less tasted them," Lilly admitted, "but I can't really say that I'm sorry."

They both laughed.

"I suppose you must have kept up your correspondence with Jimmy," Annie said, "since you eventually married him."

* * * *

August 1950

Lilly bent down to pick up the stack of mail on the entryway floor. What was it this time? Three days' worth? Four? She wasn't sure. She had lost track of the time.

She tugged at the belt on her pink chenille bathrobe and shuffled into the den. She hadn't been in here—at least she thought she hadn't been in here, since the crash—her mother's knitting was still sitting there on the sofa where she had left it. A newspaper several weeks old still lay across her father's chair. She moved the paper aside and sat down, trying to imagine she was a little girl again and that she was curled up in her daddy's lap.

She didn't cry. She was all cried out, at least for now. She just sat there, hands full of unopened mail, too tired to think. Finally, mostly because she was tired of holding them, she began looking through the letters. Sympathy cards. She could tell by the shape and the thickness. It had been almost three weeks. Everyone who had known her parents would have heard by now. At least they hadn't sent flowers. Or maybe they had. She didn't answer the doorbell these days, or the telephone, so she wouldn't really know who had called or come by. She wasn't sure if the milkman even came anymore.

She pulled out the envelopes that looked like they contained bills and put them on the coffee table. She had to take care of business matters, whatever else she did. She pulled out a notice for her class reunion and tossed it into the trash can. She was tempted to throw the sympathy cards in after it, but that wouldn't be very considerate. Her mother would have wanted her to be considerate.

She stopped. There, between the gas bill and the invoice from the funeral home was a letter from Italy. She recognized the handwriting on the envelope and felt a pang of guilt. How many of his letters had she gotten in the past three weeks? Six? Seven? She had read them, and that was more than she could say for any other correspondence she had received during that time, but she hadn't responded. She probably should at least read this one too.

Dear Lilly,

How are you? I can't tell you how sorry I was to hear about your mother and father. Kelly Morgan heard about the train crash from his girl back in Stony Point. He thought that you would have told me about it. I guess that explains why I haven't heard from you in a while. I can't even imagine how bad you must be hurting right now. I wish I was there to take care of you. I wish I was there to just hold you tight and make everything better. I don't know how, but I would. For you, Lil, I would. Please let me take care of you now. I promise I'll do everything in the world to make you happy again. Please marry me.

Love forever,
Jimmy

She sat there in her father's big chair and didn't move for the longest time. *Daddy is gone,* she thought. *Mom is gone. Peter has been gone for a long time now. They aren't coming back. None of them.* Maybe part of her had thought if she stayed here in Stony Point—if she stayed with her parents, if she didn't change from the girl she had been when Peter went off to war—he would eventually come back. If she waited long enough.

But he wasn't coming back.

None of them were.

She was on her own now. There was nothing left for her here but memories, and she thought now that she might drown in them. She *would* drown in them if she didn't get away. Italy was away. Jimmy was a soldier. Soldiering meant away—France, England, Korea, Japan, the Philippines. There was a world out there, a world she had always wanted to see. And here there was absolutely nothing left to hold her.

She wiped her face on the fleecy sleeve of her bathrobe, realizing for the first time that she was crying, and then she looked again at the stack of sympathy cards. For each one, she'd send a brief note of appreciation, and then she'd throw them away. First, though, she had a telegram to send. She didn't bother to write it out ahead of time. It was only four words.

When can I come?

~ 8 ~

"Ten days later, I had the house sold, some keep-sakes boxed away in storage and was headed across the Atlantic."

Annie squeezed Lilly's hand. "What a shock it must have been to lose your parents like that."

Lilly smiled sadly. "It was their first trip together since they were married. Can you believe it? Daddy had been saving up for the trip for a long time."

"I'm so sorry. How awful that must have been for you."

"I was only twenty-four, nearly twenty-five, and so terribly sheltered. Jimmy was a godsend to me then. He was just what I needed to keep me from going out of my mind. I loved him for that. The best thing I could have done right then was to marry him and get away from Stony Point."

"I don't blame you. I think I would've done the same thing."

"A fresh start was exactly what I needed." Lilly smiled at Annie. "I left everything behind except what I could carry in a suitcase. We were married in Rome and spent our honeymoon in Venice."

Annie sighed. "Oh, that sounds lovely. I always wanted to see Venice."

"After that, we went all over the world. We were stationed in France and England and Japan. We finally ended up in Guam and stayed there after Jimmy retired. I didn't come back to the States until he passed away eleven years ago." Lilly's eyes twinkled. "As you might think, things had changed here over that fifty years. Even in dear old Stony Point. But it was still the place I loved."

"Wow! You've really been all around the world."

Lilly laughed. "I guess I have. And it's been fun too. I'm glad ... I'm glad I didn't just stay in Stony Point and grow old by myself. Jimmy was a good husband and a wonderful father. Peter was wiser than he knew, telling me to go on with my life if he didn't come back."

"I think it showed how much he must have loved you too. Unselfishly."

"A lot of men wouldn't have wanted that, but he was never that way. And I would have hated to miss out on having children. My daughters are Army wives and still live overseas, but my son wasn't interested in the service. He wanted to live in the States, so we sent him to my old school, the University of Maine in Augusta. Now he's an office manager in an accounting firm. Between the three of them, I have eight grandchildren."

"Grandchildren!" Annie giggled. "I have two myself—twins, a boy and a girl. I don't know of anything more fun."

"Only one thing," Lilly told her. "*Great*-grandchildren. I have nineteen of those."

"Oh, my. How wonderful!'"

"And, of course, my first great-great is on the way."

Annie shook her head in amazement. "I hope you'll let me know when the baby gets here. I'd sure like to go visit the nursery."

"I'll do that, certainly."

"Where does Carl live?"

"Just over in Medomak." Lilly beamed at her. "And my great-granddaughter and her husband live there too. I'll be able to see the new baby all the time."

"That's wonderful," Annie said. She glanced at her watch. "Well, I think I've taken up enough of your time. Would you like me to leave this stuff with you now? Or have you had enough of it?" Annie gestured to the box. "I can still keep it for you if you want."

Lilly's smile was almost shy. "It's kind of a big box for just a few things, isn't it? Do you think—?" She looked around, smiling when her eyes settled on a heavy cardboard hatbox on her end table. It had decoupage of Victorian hearts and flowers. "Do you think that record would fit in there?"

Annie laid the Andrews Sisters record on the box lid. "It's a perfect fit. There's even a little room to spare. You don't happen to have a turntable, do you?"

Lilly grinned as she opened the box and took out a wide brimmed red hat with a purple ribbon and silk flower on it. "I do, but I'm afraid it doesn't play seventy-eights." She handed the hat to Annie. "Would you mind putting that in my closet? Then we can see how much of this stuff will fit in here."

"That's cute," Annie said as she stored it in the top of the neatly arranged hall closet. "Are you a Red Hat Lady?"

Lilly laughed. "Not really. The hat was a present from one of my granddaughters. I've been on a few Red Hat outings, and it is fun, but I've gotten to be such a homebody since I came back to the States. I guess after a lifetime of new people and new places, I'm just eager for peace and quiet."

She laid the record in the bottom of the hatbox and then started packing the other mementoes on top of it. For the first time, she noticed the diary.

"Oh." She picked up the little red leather book, tracing one finger over the numbers embossed in gold on the front. There was a faint blush on her cheeks. "Oh, I had forgotten you told me this was in here."

Annie bit her lip. "I did read some of it, Lilly. I'm sorry."

Lilly looked down, smiling faintly, still blushing. "What silly things we write down when we're young."

Annie put one arm around her. "No, really. It was all very sweet. You made me want to cry when you talked about how much you missed Peter and how worried you were for him. It was so honest and beautiful. There's absolutely nothing in there to be embarrassed about."

Lilly fumbled with the key and then managed to unlock the diary. She flipped it open, stopping here and there, smiling at what she saw. Then she got to December 19. The page was blank.

"What happened, Lilly?" Annie asked. "You wrote in your diary every day that year, but on the 19th of December, you just stopped."

"That was ..." She stroked her fingers across the empty lines. "That was the day I found out Peter wasn't coming back. I just didn't have anything else to say after that." She shuffled through the pages again and then opened it roughly halfway through. "Oh, here's where I turned eighteen." She laughed softly. "I mentioned getting my new camera, 'I'm sure I'll never figure out how to make it work right,' and talk about what Peter and I did when he was home on furlough. 'He laughs at me every time I try to take a picture.'" She turned a few pages, and her smile faded. "'When the war is over and he comes back, I'm never going to let him out of my sight again.'"

Annie didn't say anything. She just listened.

There was a faraway look in Lilly's eyes. "If I had known that would be the last time I saw him—" She shook her head, laughing at herself. "Well, I *am* a silly old lady, aren't I? You'd think I did nothing for the past seventy years but pine for Peter Lambert."

Annie smiled. "Of course not. Obviously you've had a busy life and a happy one."

"I have." She took a tissue from her sweater pocket and dabbed her eyes. "I'm not sorry for any of it. I don't know why all this old stuff should still affect me this way."

"I think you and Peter must have had something very special, even if it was brief. That's nothing to be ashamed of."

Lilly patted Annie's hand. "You're sweet to indulge me. I know my family would never understand. And really, this doesn't have anything to do with them, does it?"

"Not at all," Annie assured her. "Now why don't we see how much of this stuff we can get into your hatbox."

With a little finagling, they managed to get most of Lilly's mementoes stashed away and put on the lid.

"If you don't mind, just leave the rest. I'll find a smaller box for it," Lilly said. "I'm glad to finally get this all out of your way."

"I didn't mind in the least. If you ever saw Gram's

attic, you'd see this stuff was just a drop in the bucket." She straightened up what was left in the box, not looking at Lilly for a minute. "Do you still want to know what happened to him? To Peter?"

Finally she did look up. Lilly was staring at the diary that still lay in her lap.

"I don't know." Her voice quavered. "I guess it doesn't matter really. But sometimes I think—"

Annie waited.

"Sometimes I think I don't want to know, Annie. But now I wonder if that's why I haven't been able to let him go after all this time. If I only knew what really happened to him, like I do with my parents and with Jimmy, then maybe I could lay him to rest once and for all."

"I've been thinking that I'd like to find out, Lilly." Annie gave her a hopeful smile. "My friends will tell you I like poking my nose into anything I'm wondering about, and I'm wondering about what happened to Peter too. I've tried to do a little bit of looking into it already, and I'm afraid I haven't found out much at all. But would you like me to see what I can do?"

Lilly's eyes shone with hope. "Do you think you could?"

"I can't promise anything. But I'll give it my best. Do you mind if I hang on to one of his pictures for a little while—the one of him on his front porch? It might come in handy while I'm doing my research."

"Not at all." Lilly gave her an impulsive hug and then found the photo for her. "I would be so very grateful if you could find out anything about what happened to him. Can we keep this just between you and me though? Carl—I just don't think my son would understand why this is important to me."

"Of course," Annie promised as she slipped the picture into her purse. "I won't say a word."

* * * *

On her way home, Annie stopped by Town Hall, but Ian wasn't in.

"He said he had some things to see to at the mill," Mrs. Nash said, "and then he was heading home. His cable went out, so they're supposed to replace his receiver or something. Is there something I can do for you?"

"No, I'll just give him a call. Thanks."

Annie waved and went back to her car. A few seconds later, she had Ian on the phone. He sounded only slightly annoyed about the cable.

"Yeah, you know how it is," he said. "They give you a four-hour window, but you never know which part of that four hours they'll actually be using."

She chuckled. "What happened anyway?"

"I don't know. I watched the game last night and little bit of the news and went to bed. Everything was fine. I turned it on this morning to check the weather and nothing—a totally black screen."

"Awww, I'm sorry," Annie said. "Mrs. Nash said you have to have a new receiver."

"Yeah, that's what they say. I don't care what they do as long as they get everything running again. March Madness is about to start, and I don't want to miss anything."

"I'm sure they'll get you all fixed up this afternoon. But I'm glad you're home. I was hoping I could come see you."

"Oh, really?" His voice was noticeably brighter. "Can you keep me company while I wait?"

"Maybe," she said. "For a little while anyway, if you like. I was hoping you'd do me a favor."

"Sure thing. What do you need?"

"Well, we decided on an 'Easter at Grandma's' theme for the Easter banquet, with everything as vintage-looking as we can manage—kind of mix-and-match, you know? I was hoping you had some dishes and maybe some flatware we could borrow. We'll make sure and keep a record of anything you loan us and try our best to get it all back to you in mint condition. But I can't guarantee anything, so don't give me anything you couldn't stand losing."

"Ummm." He thought for a moment. "Yeah, I guess you ought to come see if anything I have will fit the bill. Are you coming now?"

"If that's all right with you. You sure you don't mind?"

"No, that would be great," he told her. "I'm sure you'll beat the cable guy here."

*   *   *   *

Ian's house was a graceful and well-kept grande dame of a house over a century old, and Annie thought it was rather like its owner: solid and reliable and blessed with classic good looks. She smiled as she drove up the long driveway and came to a stop at the front door. Ian was already standing in the door waiting for her.

"Annie!" He came out and opened the car door, offering his hand to help her out. "I told you that you'd get here first."

"No cable guy yet? I'm sorry." She followed him through the foyer and into the living room. "And you can't even watch TV while you wait for him."

He laughed and led her into the kitchen. "No, but I've been busy since you called. Tell me if any of this works for the Easter banquet."

Almost all of the whitewashed cabinet doors were open, displaying a variety of china and dinnerware.

"Wow." Annie was a little unsure where to start first. "I didn't know you had this much stuff."

He shrugged. "Arianna loved this kind of thing. I don't know. A dish is a dish to me. I'm more interested in what's in it than what's painted on it. I pretty much use these stoneware ones when I'm at home."

He pointed out some plain cream-color dishes with a teal stripe running around the rim—sturdy, no-nonsense, man's dishes. But Annie was drawn to the floral-patterned bone china that was in the cabinet next to the refrigerator.

"Oh, that's beautiful. I bet it's Royal Doulton." She took down one of the plates and turned it over. "I thought so. Gorgeous."

Ian beamed at her. "You want me to pack them up for you?"

She laughed and shook her head. "I wouldn't dream of it. I'd feel awful if any of it got broken." She looked through some of the other cabinets and found some pretty dishes with windmills and little Dutch girls on them. "How about these? They're cute and vintage-looking, but I don't think they're worth much."

"I'll trust your judgment," he said, taking an empty box from the table and putting it on the counter beside her. "Do we need to wrap them up, or will they be OK just in the box?"

"I think just the box will be OK. I'll be careful with them."

She peeked into the other open cabinets and found some other likely candidates for the banquet. Ian put them into the box for her as she continued to investigate. Then she stopped to admire some dishes that were put up on one of the upper shelves.

"Aren't these lovely?"

The pattern was floral, like most of the dishes Arianna had collected, but these were very delicate looking, airy and fresh as spring breezes and just as sweet. She knew what they must be before he said anything.

"That was our wedding pattern." He smiled a little wistfully. "I don't know much about dishes, but I know those. I kind of wish now that we had gone ahead and used them more often."

"You never did?"

"Very rarely. Arianna wanted to keep them nice, for special occasions."

"That's too bad." She gave his arm a little squeeze. "They are beautiful though—just right for a bride. I can tell she loved them."

He didn't say anything for a minute, and then he put the last of the dishes Annie had selected into the box.

"You know, Annie, I was thinking about what we talked about at the Fish House the other day." He smiled slightly. "Or I guess I should say what we *didn't* talk about."

"I don't know," Annie said. "We kind of did, didn't we?"

He took her hand and sat her down at the kitchen table and then took the chair next to her.

"We talked about talking about it. We didn't actually talk about it."

She could feel the tightness in her smile. Why should this be such a big step? He wasn't asking her to marry him. He only wanted them to move into the "this might be serious" portion of the relationship. It wasn't as if they had just met. It wasn't as if either of their spouses had just died. Why couldn't she—

"I'm not asking you to do anything but think about what you want to do. I know you loved Wayne. I loved Arianna. We've both had our times of grief. I just want you to consider that maybe it's time to move on now."

"Maybe." She shrugged. "Maybe it is. And you know, I'm not grieving anymore. I like my life here. I'm happy. I just don't ..." She shrugged again.

"Is it me?" he asked finally, and his expression was so uncertain and vulnerable, she had to look away.

"No. Of course it isn't you." She pressed her lips together and looked up at him again. "I'm just not sure, OK? And I can't give you a particular date and time saying when I will be. Maybe I never will be. I really care for you, Ian. I like what we have now. We can date, laugh, have a good time. You're one of my best friends, and I don't know if I want to risk that with something more serious."

Ian looked down. "I understand. But Annie—" He broke off when the doorbell rang, and she stood up.

"That'll be your cable guy," Annie said. "I'd better go."

He got up too, following her to the door with the box of dishes. "Look, Annie, I didn't mean to upset you. I didn't mean—"

She took the box from him and gave him a light kiss on the cheek. She let the kiss linger a moment. "It's all right, Ian. I just need to think things through, OK?"

He put his hand on the doorknob, ready to open it for her. "I'll call you later, all right?"

She looked into his anxious dark eyes, debating with herself, and then she shook her head. "Just give me some time to think."

He nodded and opened the door for her. Annie slipped past the man from the cable company and made a quick getaway.

~9~

As Annie was driving home, her cellphone rang, and she gave the caller ID a quick glance. C BERGSTROM. That could be Lilly's son. She hoped there wasn't anything wrong.

"Hello?"

"Hi, Annie. This is Carl Bergstrom. I got your number from my mother, and I hope you don't mind me giving you a call."

"Of course I don't mind. Is your mother all right?"

"Oh, don't worry. There's nothing serious going on, but …" Carl paused. "Look, Annie, I'll get right to the point. I just left my mother's place. She didn't want to tell me at first, but I found out she's been crying over that stuff you took over to her."

Annie didn't say anything. She didn't know what to say. "I—I'm sorry. I certainly didn't mean to upset her."

"No, I know you didn't mean to, but she is upset all the same. I really think it would be best if you wouldn't bring that kind of thing up to her. The past is over and done with. No use raking it all up now."

Annie pursed her lips and wished he had picked some other time to get into this.

"But she seemed so happy to see it all again," she said, struggling to keep the frustration and disappointment out of her voice. "What could it hurt—"

Carl's heavy sigh caused a little burst of static over her phone. "Look, I know you mean well, Annie. I can appreciate that. And I know Mom enjoys having visitors, but I have to ask you to let me decide what's best for her. She's not so young anymore. I'm sure you'd feel really bad if you got her all worked up over these old memories, and then she had a heart attack or something."

Annie pressed her lips together. "Yes, of course, that would be awful. Does your mother have heart problems?"

"No," he said, and she was sure there was a touch of reluctance in his voice. "No, but she's not young anymore. I just don't think it's good for her to get upset like this."

Annie tried to put herself into his shoes, even if they were rather overprotective ones. "I understand. What do you want me to do?"

"I just—I just think it would be a good idea if you didn't talk to her about the war or that guy anymore." He sounded uncertain, embarrassed. "She likes you. I can tell. And I'm sure she'd love for you to come visit. I think that'd be great. But no more of this stuff from the old days, OK?"

No wonder Lilly had wanted her to keep the stuff about Peter to herself. She obviously knew her son was a worrier. Annie took a deep breath and put a determined smile into her voice. "Carl, you know your mother is a grown woman. Shouldn't she be the one to decide what she does and doesn't want to talk about?"

"I'm asking you as a favor. Just don't bring this up to Mom again, all right?"

Annie exhaled heavily. "All right. I won't bring it up.

But if she wants to talk about it, I'm not going to deny her that. Agreed?"

"Fair enough." He suddenly sounded more relaxed. "Sorry to sound like such an ogre about this, but you know how it is. I only have one mom."

With an apology for having bothered her, Carl hung up, and Annie put her phone back into her purse. She could tell Lilly wanted to know about Peter, but had she really been that upset? Upset enough to cry for an hour or more after Annie had gone?

She blinked her eyes hard and stared out at the road ahead. She didn't need any extra stress right now. She just needed to go home and have a quiet cup of coffee and some time alone. She needed to figure out what to do about Ian. Why did he have to be so nice and so reasonable and so attractive? Maybe she needed to put the brakes on finding out about Peter Lambert too. She hated the thought of giving up, but she probably wasn't going to be able to find out anything more about him anyway. A little time to herself—that was just what she needed.

There was a hint of a smile on her face as she turned down Ocean Drive, and then her face fell. "No, no, no!"

Alice was standing on the front porch of the carriage house waving at her. She really didn't feel like company now, but there was really nothing she could do but try to get through it as quickly as possible.

Annie smiled and waved back. Then she got out of the car and went around to the passenger side to get the box of dishes. She wasn't sure how she felt about having them now.

"Ooh, what did you get?" Alice called as she scurried over to Annie's driveway. "Anything good?"

Annie let her look into the box. "More dishes for the banquet. I think I ended up with about six different kinds. Just a few pieces of each, of course, but they're cute. There are some with butterflies on them, which I think is great for Easter. Some of them are kind of harvest-y, but they're homey looking, so I think they'll do."

"Oh, those are great. Where'd you get them?"

"Ian's."

Annie tried to be nonchalant, but she could tell by the change in Alice's expression that she had failed.

"You look upset, Annie. What's the matter?"

"Is it that obvious?"

Alice gave her an understanding little smile. "Only to somebody who really knows you. Want to talk about it?"

Annie shook her head and then nodded toward Grey Gables. "Want some coffee?"

So much for thinking things out alone. But, she realized, she really didn't want to be alone. She wanted to—needed to—talk things through with someone. Alice would certainly understand. Maybe Alice could help her figure out why this was so difficult for her right now.

They went into the kitchen. Annie put the box of dishes on the counter with the ones she had gathered already and then started a pot of coffee. Alice didn't say anything. She just pulled a chair up to the table and waited until the coffee was ready.

Finally, Annie poured them each a cup and sat down

next to Alice. "I was surprised Ian had all those dishes. I guess Arianna must have been a bit of a collector."

Alice smiled. "And being a man, Ian probably uses only the same two or three all the time. Am I right?"

"Yes." Annie laughed faintly. "He told me exactly that. I guess he keeps all of these because of her."

"That's sweet." Alice's blue eyes were warm. "He's a good man."

Annie nodded, looking into the dark depths of her coffee cup. "He is a good man. A kind man, an honest man, a smart man, a gentle man, and a very attractive man." She sighed. "Why can't I make up my mind about my relationship with him? I thought we had already dealt with all of this. We've been on a few dates. I don't know if this whole thing with Lilly and Peter is making me crazy remembering about Wayne and me. I just don't know."

Alice laughed. "So that's what this is about."

"Exactly."

Alice tilted her head a little to one side. "Did you kids have a fight?" she asked, jokingly.

"No, not really. Just a talk. You know Ian. He'd never deliberately hurt anyone's feelings or do anything mean. It's nearly impossible to actually fight with him. He just thinks it's time we start thinking about where we are going."

"So, why don't you?"

"I don't know." Annie traced the rim of her coffee cup with her finger. "The last time I talked to LeeAnn, I definitely got the cold shoulder when I was talking about Ian and me going out to dinner."

"Did you find out why?"

Annie sighed. "I didn't press, but I'm pretty sure I know. She loved her daddy, and I guess it's hard for her to imagine me with another man."

"It's hardly fair of her to expect you to stay single for the rest of your life." Alice shook her head. "I mean, look at Lilly Bergstrom. She's what? Eighty-seven? Eighty-eight? You could be around for another forty years. Maybe more."

Annie chuckled. "Lilly's part of the problem too."

"Lilly? Really?"

"Well, not Lilly actually. But her son called me, and more or less told me to stop talking to his mother about the war and about Peter Lambert. He said it upset her too much."

Alice frowned. "I didn't think she was all that upset. She looked pretty interested in finding out more, if you ask me."

"I thought so too," Anne said. "But he said she had been crying ever since I left her apartment, and he didn't want her to have a heart attack or something." She shrugged. "I mean, I understand him wanting to look after her. And obviously, he knows her much better than I do. But it just didn't seem like talking to her about Peter was dangerous or anything."

Alice shook her head. "That is a little strange. Are you going to quit trying to find out what happened to him?"

Annie tilted her head to one side. "Now, really, Alice. What do you think?"

Alice laughed. "Good girl. I knew you'd never give up once you were on the trail. You'll just have to be careful what you tell Lilly, I suppose. I guess grown kids can be funny about their parents."

"Yeah. LeeAnn sometimes acts like she's the mother, and I'm the daughter."

"I know it's hard for her to think of you with someone else, but you have the right to be happy too."

Annie took a slow sip of her coffee, still thinking. "I am happy. Maybe that's what I'm afraid of most. I like my life here. I don't have a lot of worries." She smiled as she felt something warm and furry rubbing against her ankles. "My cat likes me. I have good friends. And I'm not sure if I want to risk losing one of my best friends by venturing into a romance with him. Stony Point is a very small town. If we started dating and it didn't work out, it could make things really awkward between him and me and in front of every-body we know."

"And how's that friendship right now?"

Annie grinned sheepishly, feeling her face turn a little warm. "Maybe not so good."

She got up and opened the pantry to retrieve a package of cat food. Boots made appreciative purring little mews as Annie poured some seafood-flavored crunchies into the cat bowl. Then she poured herself and Alice a little more coffee and sat down again.

"I told him I needed to think for a while."

Alice frowned sympathetically. "I hope you didn't tell him not to call you."

Annie winced slightly. "I did."

"Oh, boy!" Alice exclaimed "Now, of course, there's go-ing to be that uncomfortable 'how do we get things back to normal and who makes the first move' period to go through. And since you told him not to call—and you know he's too much of a gentleman to disregard your wishes—making that first move will be up to you." Alice winced. "Awkward!"

"I know. I know. See what I mean? The whole thing is a mess, and I just made it worse."

Alice gave her arm a comforting pat. "It'll be all right, I'm sure. Ian's a good guy. I can't imagine him not understanding you being a little unsure. It had to have been hard for him to even bring up the subject, knowing he was risking you turning him down."

Annie nodded. "That's the thing. I'm sure I've hurt his feelings, and now he's probably mad at me."

"No, not mad. I don't think he'd be mad. He's hurt and probably confused. But at least you didn't turn him down."

"No. I told him that I like where we are right now. And I told him I'd have to think about the rest. I guess it's only fair that I let him know one way or another."

Alice nodded. "At least try to figure out what you want."

"That's what he said. It's funny, because that's all he said. He didn't press me for any kind of a decision. He just said I ought to figure out what I want."

"Probably not a bad idea." Alice drank the last of her coffee and stood up. "I'd better get back home. I have a Divine Décor party in a little while." Alice's work as a representative of interior design products and a second line of Princessa jewelry products were what allowed her to have a flexible schedule.

She sympathetically looked at her best friend. "Annie, I know making a change, even a good one, can be scary, but love can be a really elusive thing. It doesn't always come along just when we're looking for it." There was a touch of knowing regret in her face. "Don't let being afraid spoil something that could be really good."

Annie stood up too, and gave her friend a hug. "Thanks, Alice. Thanks for letting me talk. Thanks for being there, and thanks for the reminder."

"Anytime."

Alice gave her a little wave and let herself out, leaving Annie alone with her thoughts.

*   *   *   *

The next few days passed quickly. Annie tried to get more information about what had happened to Peter Lambert, but she only hit dead end after dead end. Evidently, very few of the OSS records had survived the war. She was still waiting for answers to some of her inquiries, but so far she was getting nowhere.

She was also getting no closer to making a decision about what she wanted to do about Ian. What they had now was nice. At least it had been nice. She hadn't spoken to Ian since she had left his house. But she was sure things would eventually get back to normal, and things would be good between them again. But maybe Alice was right. Maybe there could be so much more.

Annie almost dreaded going into A Stitch in Time for the weekly meeting of the Hook and Needle Club. Not that she didn't look forward to getting together with her friends and relaxing with her crochet, but she wasn't quite in the mood for any awkward questions about Ian, or worse, any overly sympathetic glances. She knew Ian would never say anything to anyone about the little strain in their relationship, and neither would Alice, but Stony Point was a small town. If Annie didn't drop by his office from time to time, or if she and Ian didn't go out for a meal now and again, there would be talk. Well, she supposed the best thing to do would be for her to go about business as usual and not make things worse.

"I haven't seen you much around town," Mary Beth said once Annie had settled into her usual chair. "What have you been up to?"

"Oh, not much." Annie smiled and pulled out the cardigan she was working on. "My friend Lilly called to tell me her great-granddaughter had her baby this morning. And I'm still trying to find some information about my World War II soldier and trying to get ready for the banquet. How are all of you doing finding plates and flatware we can borrow?"

"My grandmother loaned me her dishes," Peggy said. "They're ones her grandmother got at the movie theater one time in the 1930s in between the features. They asked which lady had the most kids, and my great-great-grandmother won because she had ten."

They all laughed.

"Those are antiques," Gwen said. "Are you sure it's OK if we use them?"

"Oh, Grandma doesn't mind. They're not worth much except as a family curiosity. There are some serving dishes that go with them too. Oh, thanks." Peggy took the spool of thread Mary Beth brought her and compared it to the leaf she was appliquéing onto her quilt block. "That's just the right color. Remind me to pay you before I leave, OK?"

"Sure thing," Mary Beth assured her, sitting down with the rest of the ladies. "What about you, Annie? I borrowed my neighbor's old cut-glass plates and some antiques for the tables. Have you had any luck?"

"I saw Mrs. Nash at the bank the other day," Gwen said before Annie could respond. "She told me you were going to borrow some dishes from Ian. I guess he's been pretty busy lately too."

Gwen was concentrating on turning the toe on the sock she was knitting and didn't see the other women glance at each other. Annie didn't miss it. Obviously they had all noticed the sudden coolness between her and Ian.

Suddenly, Gwen looked up at Annie, just realizing what she had said. "I mean, he hasn't been around town much. Not that I've seen. I just, um … wondered."

"I imagine he stays pretty busy," Anne said, making her voice bright. "You know, with the mill and all."

"Speaking of serving dishes," Alice put in quickly, "have we settled on what our menu is going to be?"

They began to debate the merits of ham versus turkey, and Annie blessed Alice for her perceptiveness. She would definitely be glad when the meeting was over.

— 10 —

The awkwardness at A Stitch in Time had quickly passed, but Annie couldn't help thinking about it as she walked back down Main Street to where she had parked her car. She was startled when she heard a soft voice behind her.

"Hello, Annie."

She froze where she was, and then, with a taut smile, she turned around. "Hello, Ian. How are you?"

"Sorry I haven't talked to you for a while; that's how I am."

She pursed her lips, trying not to smile. "Oh, really?"

"Really. Will you come have a cup of coffee with me?"

She glanced at her watch as if she were pressed for time. "I really should—"

"I come bearing gifts." He held up a manilla envelope. "One of our senators is a personal friend of mine. He had some of his people do a little checking with the War Department. I think you'll be interested in what they found out."

She couldn't help an excited little catch in her breath, and then she shook her head. "That doesn't change my mind you know. It's very nice of you to have done this for me, but you know I still don't—"

"Annie, please. Didn't you say you like where we are— or at least were? Come have coffee with me and let me show you what I found out. OK?"

Annie finally smiled again. "You're too nice for your own good, Ian Butler. I hope you know that."

They walked over to The Cup & Saucer, the small diner where Peggy Carson worked next door to A Stitch in Time, and sat in the back booth—their usual booth—and Peggy came over to take their order, giving Annie a knowing little smile behind Ian's back.

"What'll it be, folks?"

"Just coffee, Peg," Annie said.

"Me too, thanks," Ian added.

Once Peggy was gone, he put the envelope on the table and didn't say anything.

"You found out something about Peter Lambert?" she asked finally.

He nodded. "Evidently there aren't that many records about covert operations back then. I guess that makes sense. But of course, they do keep records when someone gets the Purple Heart."

Annie smiled. "They gave him the Purple Heart?"

"For being wounded in action. Evidently he was meant to blow up a munitions factory and didn't get away in time."

"What a shame. In 1943?"

"Yes," Ian said, "but get this. He didn't get the Purple Heart until 1992."

Annie frowned in thought. "Almost fifty years later? Why'd it take them so long? Did someone finally bring him to the attention of the War Department?"

"Yep."

"I didn't think he had any family left. Who would it have been?"

Ian grinned. "The old boy himself."

"What?" Annie blinked at him, open-mouthed. "He was still alive in '92?"

"Evidently." Ian smiled at her, a gleam in his dark eyes. "I remember hearing the story back then, but I had forgotten about it in the past twenty years or so."

"What story?" Annie grabbed the envelope and opened it up, spreading the papers on the table. "You knew about this?"

"Maybe you'll remember it too, when you hear the details. The soldier who was believed killed but had been in East Germany all along and couldn't get out until the Berlin Wall came down?"

"Wait a minute. I do remember that story. I thought it was really amazing that it had taken him so long to get home. Hard to believe."

Ian grinned. "Truth is stranger than fiction, they say."

"And that was Peter Lambert?"

"The one and only. I just wonder that Lilly didn't know about it. It was quite a sensation at the time, for a little while at least."

"I don't know where she would have been twenty years ago. Guam, I think she said. She and her husband lived all over the world after the war. She's—" Annie broke off, smiling as Peggy brought their coffee and then, taking the hint, retreated. "She's only been back in the U.S. for the past eleven years."

"But wouldn't news like that have been big on an Army base?" Ian asked. "Even in Guam?"

"Probably, but her husband was retired by then. She told me they kept pretty much to themselves at that point. I guess after a lifetime in the Army, he was ready to get away from all that."

"Maybe so." Ian nodded toward the papers he had brought. "I'm afraid most of this is about the red tape involved in getting him back to the States and back into his right name, and finally, getting him his Purple Heart. Seems he was rather reluctant to have any sort of recognition. He just wanted to come home."

Annie looked over everything again, shaking her head. "Wow. Nearly fifty years. It's—I don't even know what it is. It's amazing. It's heartbreaking. His whole life, really, just snatched from him like that."

Ian nodded sympathetically. "It is a shame, but at least he did finally make it home. A lot of boys back then never did."

Annie's smile was tinged with sadness. "You're right. How terrible it must have been though." She turned one of the pages. "Did they say where he is now?"

"No, I'm afraid not. Those records are all from '92. But at least now you know he was alive then. You should be able to track down where he's living, if he still is."

"After more than twenty years?" She pursed her lips. "He's more likely passed on than not. But if Lilly's still with us, I guess there's no reason he couldn't be too—right?"

He grinned. "Worth checking into, if you ask me."

"Thank you, Ian." She hesitated a moment and then reached over and took his hand. "And I'm sorry I snapped at you the other day."

A little color crept into his cheeks, and he looked down into his coffee cup. "I guess I can be a little pushy sometimes."

"And I guess I overreact when I'm feeling stressed."

He squeezed her hand. "I didn't mean to pressure you."

She sighed. "You didn't. I mean, OK, maybe a little, but not really. I've been dancing around the issue for a long time now. It's not unreasonable of you to want an answer of some kind."

"And it's not unreasonable of you to not want to be pushed into a decision you're not ready for. I shouldn't have to be reminded of that. Any pushing at this point would only push us apart."

With another squeeze, she released his hand. "I told you you were too nice for your own good. You don't know how much I appreciate you finding this out for me." She put the papers back into the envelope. "Is it OK if I make a copy of this and bring it back later?"

"That's yours. You're the interested party. I'm only here to help."

"What can I do to repay the favor?" she asked as she stowed the envelope in her bag. "Buy you lunch?"

He looked for a minute as if he might protest, but then he smiled. "That would be great."

Things were pretty much back to normal by the time Annie and Ian finished their burgers and fries. She still didn't know if she was ready to move wholeheartedly into romance, but she did enjoy his company, and she realized more than ever just how much she had missed him the past few days.

"Thank you again for getting this information for me," Annie said. "Lilly will be thrilled to know Peter was awarded the Purple Heart."

"Do you suppose he's still around?"

"I plan to find out as soon as I get home. How many Peter Lamberts his age can there be?"

Ian nodded. "I'm interested now. You know, you could come back over to the office with me for a minute and look it up."

Annie grinned at him. "That's a great idea."

Back at Town Hall, Annie and Ian discovered that there were nine pages worth of Peter Lamberts and P. Lamberts, and seven of the men were listed as being sixty-five or older.

Annie frowned as she leaned over his desk and scanned the list. "They're all over the country, aren't they?"

"Yeah." Ian said. "Pennsylvania, Arizona, Florida. Wait a minute. Friendship? Friendship, Maine? No way."

"You're kidding." Annie laughed and squinted at the computer screen. "There's a Peter Lambert in Friendship? Is there a number listed?"

There was.

Annie looked at Ian, hardly able to keep the grin off her face. "Do you think I should call?"

He shrugged. "I guess you'll never know if it's him unless you do."

"Oh, I can't believe it." She couldn't help the tremor in her voice. "If it is the right Peter Lambert—and if he agrees, of course—would you go with me to talk to him? I'd hate to go alone."

"I'd love to talk to him. He's got quite a story to tell, and I'd really like to hear it firsthand." An encouraging gleam in his eyes, Ian pushed the telephone from his side of the desk over to hers. "Go ahead."

She punched in the number and felt her heartbeat speed up as it rang. Finally, there was a click.

"Hello?"

Annie swallowed hard and glanced at Ian. Here goes. "Is this Mr. Lambert? Mr. Peter Lambert?"

"Yes. May I ask who's calling, please?"

His voice was low and still steady. It wasn't a young man's voice, but it didn't have the quaver of old age either. Could she be actually speaking to Peter Lambert? Lilly's Peter Lambert? She took a deep breath and plunged ahead.

"You don't know me, Mr. Lambert, but my name is Annie Dawson. I'm doing some research, and I was wondering if you are the Peter Lambert who lived at 305 Maple in Stony Point in 1943."

"Yes, I did. That was quite a while ago. Is there something I can do for you?"

"I was wondering if you had time to talk to me about your experiences in the war and afterward."

He didn't say anything for the longest time.

"Mr. Lambert?"

"I'm sorry. Mrs. Dawson, did you say?"

"Yes."

"I'm sorry, Mrs. Dawson." He laughed softly. "I guess you caught me a little off guard. It's been a long, long time since anybody wanted to talk to me about the war."

"I suppose you had a lot of reporters bothering you when you got your Purple Heart."

Annie couldn't help feeling a little bit sorry for him. If he had been as self-effacing as Lilly remembered, all that attention must have been torture for him.

"A few," he admitted. "What is it you want to know?"

"Is it possible for you to meet me somewhere? I'd be

happy to come to you, if that would be better. I have a picture I think you'd like to see."

"A picture? Of what?"

"Of you." Annie couldn't help smiling as she said it. "I think you must have been about eighteen."

He laughed again. He had a very nice laugh—a warm, friendly sort of laugh.

"I guess you'd better come see me. Do you mind coming to my place?"

"Not at all. You're in Friendship—right?"

"Goodness," he said. "Everybody knows everything about everybody these days. Yes, that's right. Where are you coming from?"

"Stony Point."

"OK. Come straight down the Waldoboro Road into Friendship. My apartment building is called Ocean View Haven, off Martin Point Road. I'm in number 504."

"If you don't mind, I'd like to bring a friend of mine along with me. He remembers hearing about you when you got your Purple Heart, and he'd love to meet you."

Peter chuckled. "Ummm, yes, I suppose. The more the merrier. When did you want to come? I don't have any plans this afternoon."

"Say about an hour?" Annie looked at Ian for his approval, and he gave her a quick nod. "Would that work?"

"See you in an hour then, Mrs. Dawson."

～ 11 ～

Ocean View Haven was an apartment complex for people fifty-five and over. Apartment 504 was across from the leasing office but facing a little wooded patch at the back of the complex.

"Looks like he's got a nice view," Ian said as they waited for Peter to answer the door. "I think if I'd been through everything he has, I'd want some peace and quiet too."

"I guess he's doing pretty well healthwise if he's living here on his own. I'm so glad." Annie beamed at Ian. "I still can't believe we're actually going to talk to him. Lilly will be amazed."

"Better get a little more information, Annie, before you start planning the big reunion. Seventy years is a long time. People change. Maybe he doesn't want to see her now. It's been twenty years. If he were going to look her up, wouldn't he have done it by now? Could be he fell in love with someone else a long time ago—maybe more than once."

Before Annie could reply to that, the doorknob rattled, and then the door swung open.

"Mr. Lambert?"

He was still tall, as lanky as he had been when he was in uniform, and his eyes were an almost-impossible shade of sky blue. His hair was white rather than blond now, and he leaned on a cane, but he was still a remarkably handsome man, especially when he smiled.

"You must be Mrs. Dawson."

Annie offered him her hand. "Call me Annie, please. This is my friend, Ian Butler."

"It's an honor to meet you, sir," Ian said, shaking the older man's hand, and Peter grinned self-consciously.

"Well, come in, Annie, Ian. And you'd both better call me Peter."

The front door opened immediately to the living room. It was a cozy space lined with books. He showed them to a battered brown leather sofa. They made themselves comfortable, and he lowered himself into what was obviously his favorite recliner.

"So what can I do for you?"

Annie returned his smile and took out the picture she had borrowed from Lilly, the one showing a young Peter in uniform on the front porch of his mother's house in Stony Point.

"I think this is you."

"Well, well." He took the photo from her, pushing his bifocals up on his nose so he could get a better look. "That one was taken more than a few days ago, wasn't it? I tell you what, though, I remember when this was taken. Where in the world did you get it? I thought all of this sort of thing was long gone."

"Do you remember who took it?" Annie asked, leaning forward to look at it with him, but looking at his expression more than at the photo.

"Very well." A wistful tenderness came into his eyes, and more and more, Annie could see that smiling young soldier in him.

"Do you mind telling me who it was?"

"Proud to. Her name was Lilly Pryce, and we were going to get married after the war was over."

"Why didn't you?"

He shrugged slightly. "Guess it wasn't meant to be. When I finally got home, and I suppose that took me a lot longer than either of us expected, I never could find her. I suppose she's gone now. I promised I'd come back to her, and I couldn't keep that promise. I tried, Annie, I swear, but I just never could."

Annie glanced at Ian. "Do you know where I got that picture, Peter?"

The older man shook his head.

"It's a little bit of a long story. I inherited my house in Stony Point from my grandmother. Gram left all kinds of stuff up in her attic, and a few days ago I came across a box with some things from the war in it, some letters and pictures and things. This was one of them."

"Who was your grandmother? It wasn't—"

"Her name was Betsy Holden, but I don't think you ever met her."

Peter only shook his head again. "How in the world did my things get in her attic?"

"She was a friend of Lilly's. She was storing those things for her."

"For—for Lilly? Is she—" His hand shook, and he suddenly removed his glasses, wiping them on his shirt. "Is she still alive?"

"She's living in Bremen right now." Annie put her hand over his. "Are you all right?"

"She—" He dropped his head, but not before she saw there were tears in his eyes. "She is?"

Annie beamed at him. "She is."

"I looked for her. For years, I looked for her. And she's been just across the bay over in Bremen all this time?"

"After I found your pictures up in the attic, I tracked her down. Her name is Lilly Bergstrom now, and she's only been back in the States for the past eleven years. Maybe that's why you never found her."

"Bergstrom?" His eyes narrowed, and he smiled ruefully. "Bergstrom, eh? So Jimmy got her after all, that son of a gun."

"He died eleven years ago."

Peter nodded, his grim expression softening. "I'm glad she married. And Jimmy was a good guy. I'm sure he took good care of her. Uh, they have any kids?"

"Three, I believe. Two daughters and a son. I met the son, Carl. He seems pretty nice."

"That's good."

"His granddaughter just had a baby of her own—Lilly's great-great-grandchild—just this morning."

"Wow." Peter shook his head. "Might have been mine."

"Do you …" Annie hesitated. "Do you have any grandchildren yourself?"

He shook his head. "Never did marry. I knew Lil was the only one for me. But I'm glad she didn't spend all these years alone. That's not what I wanted for her."

"I read some articles about you receiving the Purple Heart," Ian said. "They said you ended up in East Germany after the war."

"That's right." Peter looked Ian over. "You've been in the service, or I miss my guess."

Ian nodded. "Yes, sir. Navy."

"Ah, I always admired you guys." Peter chuckled. "Buddy of mine was in the Navy. He always said he was never worried about his ship sinking because, no matter where they were, they were never more than a couple of miles from land."

"Yeah," Ian said. "Straight down."

They all laughed.

"Anyway, I don't guess you came to hear about my friends," Peter said. "And even now, I can't give you a lot of details about what happened to me. My memory is a little spotty in places."

"What happened?" Annie asked. "What do you remember?"

Peter thought for a moment. "When I was in the Army, they got me a German identity, a name, and all the papers, and then they smuggled me in. My papers showed that I had been transferred into a German unit on the French border. I had always thought it might be fun to do some espionage work, you know? I had no idea what I was getting into."

* * * *

November 1943

Peter nodded as his fellow soldier passed by, stamping the snow from his boots. As soon as he was out of sight, Peter moved over to the little stand of trees by the fence. He had exactly three minutes, he knew, before Sergeant Garber came back that way. He counted three trees to the right of the signpost and moved the bracken that covered the hollow space in the fourth. His hands shook as he reached in and removed the oilskin-wrapped package. It was heavy, and he felt his heart rate increase.

He'd been trained for this. He'd thought he was prepared. But there was no training that could really make you ready to live with the possibility of being found out as a spy and summarily shot.

There was supposed to be nothing to this. All he had to do was slide the package under the fence. Someone inside—and he wasn't told whom—would take it from there. After that, he would have until the shift changed and the workers left. His own watch would be over by then too, and he would be in *Der Drosselbart* with the rest of his mates, drinking to *der Führer's* health. Garber came back by.

"You have a cigarette, Bretz?"

Peter shook his head, making himself look particularly young and guileless. "Sorry. I don't smoke."

Garber cursed him good-naturedly. "The puppies they give us now. What use are you?"

Peter only grinned and shrugged. "Maybe Hoefler can help you."

"Eh, probably should cut down anyway."

The whistle blew, and workers started pouring out of the gates under the watchful eyes of the guards. Only a few minutes now. Another young soldier came to take Peter's place. This boy looked no older than Peter. How he wished he could warn him.

"Well, I'm off duty now," Peter told Garber, and the Sergeant sighed.

"Four hours more for me. You're going to *Der Drosselbart*?"

Peter nodded. "Where else?"

The men were always more talkative when they'd had something to drink.

Garber looked him up and down. "Elsie, is it?"

Peter blushed and looked down, glancing surreptitiously at his watch. He was running out of time. "No. She'd never be interested in me."

Garber laughed. "She likes a pretty face. Of course she'd be interested in you."

Peter shook his head. "I'm sure she's very nice. I just don't—"

"She's not going to expect anything from you, boy. Just a bit of companionship, you know."

"Really, I have to go. My friends—"

"Yes, friends." Garber winked and made a curvy outline with his hands. "So if it's not Elsie, then who—"

"Nobody. Just friends. I have to—"

The Sergeant put his arm around Peter's shoulders, still chuckling. "I see now. You have a little mädchen back in Dusseldorf or wherever you're from."

Peter managed a smile, hoping the man couldn't feel the racing of his heart through his coat. Only a few seconds left. "Yes. Yes, I do."

"And her name?"

"Lilly."

"Ah. Pretty, I suppose."

"Yes. Now, I must get going. My friends—"

"Ah, the friends again. 'Friends' are rarely so urgent." Garber did not release his hold. "Perhaps it is Elsie after all? But don't worry. Your Lilly need never know. Elsie won't tell. I won't tell. And you—"

*   *   *   *

When he woke, Peter's head was bandaged, and he couldn't hear anything but a low hum inside his head. His right leg hurt fiercely, but other than that and general body aches, he felt fit enough. He touched the bandage around his head, noting that it was especially heavy over his ears, and wondered if that was why he couldn't hear anything. He started pulling it off, and then someone grabbed his hands, holding them away from his head. A young nurse was scowling at him. He couldn't hear her, of course, but he could tell from her expression that she was scolding him.

He motioned to his ears, trying not to panic, and she patted his hands, setting them in his lap. Then she held up one finger, instructing him to wait. She took a pad from her pocket and scribbled something on it.

You just had surgery. How do you feel?

It took him a moment, and then he scrawled out his answer, his fingers oddly clumsy on the pencil. *Leg hurts. Head hurts. Where am I?*

She smiled. *Hospital. Berlin. You were in an explosion.*

He nodded. *How long ago?*

Three months.

He gaped at her, pointing at what she had written and questioning her with his eyes.

She nodded and pointed at the words herself. Then she wrote more. *What do you remember?*

He considered for another moment, the breath trembling out of him. Then he took the pencil from her again. *Nothing.*

*   *   *   *

Peter smiled at Annie. "Her name was Clara. Clara Grünewald. She looked after me while I recovered from the last of I don't know how many surgeries. I got the hearing back in my right ear after about another month, but never did in my left. I remembered nothing before I woke up that day. Not the explosion, not the three months in the hospital, nothing—not even my name. I guess it was a blessing of a sort. I couldn't possibly give myself away."

"So you didn't speak English while you recovered?" Ian asked.

"I guess, because they spoke to me in German and German was my first language more than English, I naturally thought that way. I didn't even know I spoke English until a few months later. Because of my injuries and my memory loss, they didn't send me back into the field. I ended up as a hospital orderly. Clara looked after me after that first day. But more than that, I can't tell you what happened. I'm sure parts of my memory are still gone. I never did remember the actual explosion, though obviously there was one." He tapped the hearing aid hidden behind his left ear and winked at Annie. "I don't have this just because I'm old, you know."

She smiled, her expression encouraging him to carry on with his story.

"Anyway, everything before the German hospital was gone for the longest time. They had no reason to think I was anything but Wilhelm Bretz. I couldn't remember anything before that, so I believed them when they told me who and what I was. By the time I got out of the hospital, the war was over. I thought for a while that I might ask Clara to marry me. She was three or four years older than I, but she was a nice girl and took wonderful care of me. There was just something, something in the back of my mind somewhere, that told me I wasn't free to marry anyone."

"So what did you do?" Annie asked.

"I went back to the house at the address my service records listed as my home in Berlin.

— 12 —

October, 1945

Nobody seemed to be able to tell him anything. Kurfürstenstrasse—part of Berlin's subway system— was a heap of rubble, bleak and empty. It had been bombed more than two years earlier, but so many places had. Not all of them, he'd been told, could be rebuilt at once. He found what he thought was Number 27, but he couldn't be sure of even that. Number 19 was still marked, as well as Number 30 across the road. The rest was a jumbled mass of concrete, wood, and dirt, faded by two years' worth of weather, softened with snow. He stood staring at it until a little dog rushed up to him, barking furiously until he backed away.

Michaelstrasse, northwest of his street, seemed to be in better shape, and he found himself walking along it, searching for something familiar. A house, a street corner, a face—anything. Instead, people only stared back at him, some of them sympathetic, most of them annoyed that he would look at them so searchingly and make them wonder, even briefly, if they knew him.

Finally he slowed, leaning on a lamppost to catch his breath. He stopped a young housewife, hurrying her children inside, to ask if she knew him. She only shook her head, and he thanked her and continued along the street, trying to keep from stumbling on his aching leg. He was bold enough to stop where another housewife, this one older and sterner, was shaking out a little rug from her front stoop. And then a little way down the street, a boy was standing around to the side of the last house, sneaking a smoke. Neither of them knew him or had heard of anyone called Bretz.

He pushed on to the next street, Belfortstrasse, looking into the restaurants and little shops. There were a few more people about, but they all seemed intent on getting to wherever it was they were going. Besides, it was getting colder as evening approached, and they huddled down into their overcoats and mufflers, unwilling to look up. He pulled his own coat a bit more snugly around his shoulders and held it closed at the neck.

This was no good. Nobody knew him—not here, not anymore. The doctors had told him that, God willing, at least part of his memories would come back. Still, it would be nice. ... Who was he kidding? It wasn't just nice. It was imperative. He had been someone, and he needed to know who that someone was.

He grudgingly conceded to himself that he wasn't likely to find that out just this minute, and perhaps he should be heading back to the room he had taken for the week. But, as he headed for the end of the street and toward the intersecting road, the road that would take him back to his room, the sign over the door of one of the shops caught his eyes.

Buchhandlung Walther K. Lambert.

Just a bookshop. Why had he even noticed it?

It was getting dark enough for the light from the shop windows to shine out onto the pavement, and he walked over to look inside. There was nothing remarkable about the place. It was tidy, a little bare, but none of that was uncommon. Not these days.

He leaned against the window frame, again catching his breath. His right leg was burning something fierce, and he closed his eyes, waiting for the pain to ease. They sprang open when he felt a hesitant hand at his shoulder.

The woman was middle-aged with a comfortably settled, housewifely sort of look to her and a soft roundness that said she was likely a good cook. She was saying something he couldn't quite catch, and he turned his good ear to her.

"I'm sorry?"

"I asked if you are all right."

He nodded. "Do you ... know me?"

She shook her head, looking half-puzzled and half-wary.

"Did you ever hear of Wilhelm Bretz who lives on Kurfürstenstrasse?"

"N-no. I'm sorry."

He glanced again at the sign. *Walther K. Lambert.* Did he know any Lamberts?

"You are Frau Lambert?"

She smiled. "No. I am Margarete Schoettmer. My husband, God rest his soul, bought the shop from Herr Lambert a few years before the war. Did you know the Lamberts?"

He didn't think he knew them. Why did that seem like a name he should know? He shook his head and then gave her an uncertain smile and shrugged. "I don't think so."

He made a slight bow and took a step away from the shop. But his bad leg had reached its limit, and he crashed to one knee on the pavement. She was immediately beside him, taking his arm and helping him to stand.

"Are you sure you're all right, young man? Perhaps you'd better come in and have something hot to drink."

"Really, it's nothing. I have a bit of trouble with my leg, and if I get too tired—"

"You were a soldier."

It wasn't a question.

He smiled. "There were many of us."

A ghost of pain glinted in her eyes, but she merely returned his smile and kept a firm hold on his arm.

"Come along now. It's going to get a lot colder before it gets warmer, and I'm not sending you home without something hot inside you."

She wouldn't listen to his protests, and in another minute he found himself seated at a little table in a room behind her shop with a cup of hot chocolate warming his hands and his insides. He hadn't tasted hot chocolate since … well, obviously he wasn't quite sure how long it had been, but it seemed like a very long time.

"How in the world did you get the chocolate? I thought—"

She put her finger to her upturned lips. "A certain customer of mine is as fond of American detective novels as I am of chocolate. We each use our … connections, and both of us end up happy."

He gave her the slightest hint of a grin. "It's good of you to share with a stranger."

"Ah, well." She sank into the chair across from him with a relieved sigh. "It tastes better with company if you ask me. So, tell me. Who is this Wilhelm Bretz you're looking for?"

Somehow it all spilled out of him, waking up in the hospital, not remembering anything, looking for some clue to who he was. She didn't interrupt his tale or badger him with questions. She merely listened, and when he was done, she nodded.

"The war has taken from all of us."

She got up and went into another room, a bedroom, he assumed. When she came back, she was carrying a framed photograph. It showed three fair-haired youths. Two were dressed in army uniforms, but the youngest was wearing the uniform of the Hitler Youth. They looked very starched and solemn, and he could see the woman's features in all of them.

"That's Rudy," she said, pointing to the one who must have been the oldest of them. "And that's Max and then my youngest, Dieter. I suppose he would have been about your age by now."

"Would have been?"

Her smile was brittle. "They sent him to North Africa to fight, and he never came back. He was only sixteen."

"I'm sorry."

"Of course, Rudy and Max are gone too. One in France, the other in Norway." She smiled a little more genuinely then. "You remind me a little of Dieter, you know. I don't think he'd have been so tall as you, but who knows? I would have liked to find out."

There wasn't much he could say at that point, so he only nodded, letting her decide if she wanted to say more. She left the photograph on the table and went into the shop. When she came back, she had a pair of books with her, and she looked mischievous as she set them down before him.

"I thought you might like to see what's paying for our hot chocolate this evening."

The books were by Raymond Chandler—*The Big Sleep* and *Farewell, My Lovely*, and he grinned as he picked one of them up.

"I remember these. Great stories."

Her eyes widened. "You—you read English?"

He stopped where he was. Did he?

Brows drawn together, he opened the book in his hand. *It was about eleven o'clock in the morning, mid-October, with the sun not shining ....*

"I—I suppose I can. I'm not sure why."

That slightly wary look came back into her face. "Do you speak it?"

He paused again, thinking.

"Yes," he said in English. "I guess so."

The words felt strange and yet familiar on his tongue.

"American," she observed in German. "Not British."

"Do you speak English?"

She shook her head. "No more than a few words, mostly to say I don't speak English. I wish I did though. I have many American and British soldiers in the shop these days" She thought for a moment. "You ... do you have work?"

"No, I—" He looked down, not liking to admit it. "No."

She smiled at him. "How about another cup of hot chocolate?"

*   *   *   *

Peter grinned at Annie. "It worked out pretty well for both of us. I lived behind the shop, in her son's old room, and clerked for her. I took care of the GIs who came in, and she took care of me. And if she sometimes called me Dieter rather than Wilhelm, well, I smiled and answered anyway."

"She sounds lovely."

"Yes. Yes, she was. I couldn't remember my own mother at the time, but she was like one to me."

Ian shook his head. "It's amazing, that shop having the name Lambert. I suppose that's what made you stop there."

"I think so. Of course, it's hard to say now. My memories still aren't all quite right. I did find out that those Lamberts were no relation, but Mutti Schoettmer treated me like family."

"Do you—Do you remember your own mother now?"

"Yes. Very clearly now, but it took a long time. After I left the hospital, I started having little flashes of memories. Playing hockey in the winter. A cat I used to have. Going to school. And always, a girl with big brown eyes. And it was odd, because almost all of those memories were in English, but they were infrequent and so fleeting, I could never make anything out of them. I figured I was Wilhelm Bretz from Kurfürstenstrasse, and that anything else was just my imagination."

"And you never married over there?"

Peter shook his head. "It was the darnedest thing. Mutti Schoettmer tried her best to set me up with the daughters of her friends and some of the neighborhood girls, and I was very fond of a few of them. I thought for a while that one of the girls—her name was Ivonne—I thought she might be the one for me. But I just couldn't. There was always something in the back of my mind that told me I belonged to someone else."

Annie gave him an understanding smile, and he winked at her.

"Probably for the best. Ivonne got tired of waiting on me and finally married the local butcher. By the time I left in 1990, she had nine kids and I don't know how many grandchildren."

Ian chuckled.

"It was a couple of years after the Wall went up that I really started to remember," Peter said. "I was pushing forty by then, still a little shell-shocked, I think, and wondering if I was losing my mind. But it gradually came back to me. I think I nearly gave poor Mutti Schoettmer a heart attack when I came to breakfast one morning and told her I was an American named Peter Lambert. It was about three years after that before I could tell her why I happened to be patrolling in a German uniform at the time of the explosion. We both agreed it wouldn't be a good idea for me to start telling people who I was. It was such an unlikely tale, the East Germans probably would have thought I was just making up something to get myself out of the country. And I was afraid that, if they had believed me, they wouldn't have looked too kindly on my efforts during the war."

"Wasn't there anyone you could have told?" Annie asked. "Couldn't anyone have helped you?"

"You don't know what it was like then. We were watched closely. One of the first things I learned after the Wall went up was to keep my head down and not attract attention to myself. It wasn't long after I really started remembering things that Mutti Schoettmer passed away."

"When was that?" Ian asked.

"It was 1965. I remember because it was my fortieth birthday."

Annie squeezed his hand. "I'm so sorry."

"I didn't know if my own mother was gone by then. I managed to get a letter out to her, when I remembered my old address, but nothing ever came of it. Either it was confiscated before it left the country, or it ended up in the dead-letter office."

"Lilly told me she died the year after you were believed killed."

Peter nodded. "Yes, I found that out after I got back. Poor Mutti, she was never very strong on her own. I would have hated to think of her being alone for a long time."

"But what happened after Frau Schoettmer passed on?" Ian asked. "Did you still work at the bookshop?"

"Yes. The shop was too small for the government to care much about it, though they were pretty strict about what I could sell—mostly propaganda. And the British and American soldiers weren't on our side of the Wall, of course, and speaking English wasn't of particular use anymore. But I stuck it out. And that's about it, I suppose. Once the Wall came down, I hotfooted it over to the American Consulate on the west side and told them who I was. They were pretty skeptical at first, but I finally got them to check my fingerprints against my service record." He laughed. "After that, I suppose I was kind of a celebrity. Or maybe VIP is a better description. They took mighty good care of me and got me back home quick. You know about the Purple Heart. I was interviewed a few times, but I didn't much care for that."

Annie grinned. "Lilly told me you were never much for being in the spotlight."

He ducked his head, an almost-boyish gesture, and grinned back. "She didn't tell you about that school play I was in, did she?"

"I'm afraid so."

"Oh, boy. First and last for me, I can tell you. I didn't mind the acting all that much, but that costume!"

"She said you looked gorgeous in it. 'Magnificent' is the word she used."

"She would." He shook his head in good-natured exasperation. "And my friends never let me hear the end of it."

Annie laughed. "So I guess acting wasn't something you pursued once you got back home."

"Hardly. But I got a little something from the government—back pay and disability and such. It's enough to keep me going if I'm careful. I taught German at a junior college for a while too. That gave me a little extra money to keep up my search for Lilly. But, after all those years, everything was a dead end. She had sold her house years before. Everybody who would have known her was dead or had moved away. I found records of the deaths of her mother and father, but nothing on her. No marriage records. No death record. Nothing."

"That's a tough break," Ian said. "I don't know how you could have found her. Annie told me that when her parents died, Lilly sold the house and moved to Italy. That's where she married Jimmy Bergstrom. That's why there were no marriage records for her in the U.S."

"I can't tell you how long I looked, especially after there started being records available on the internet." Peter sighed. "Nothing. You know, I thought when I got my Purple Heart that she might have heard about it and gotten in touch with me."

"She and Jimmy lived in Guam after he retired until he passed away," Annie told him. "I don't think she ever heard about you coming back. If she had, I'm sure they both would have wanted to see you."

Peter didn't say anything. He merely sat staring at nothing. Then he smiled at her again.

"So how—how is she? Lilly, I mean. Does she seem like she's happy?"

Annie squeezed his hand. "She's doing great. She has a little apartment in Bremen. And I think she's still as pretty as a picture."

He laughed faintly. "Just over in Bremen. All these years. I've got to see her."

"Well ..." Annie winced a little. "I'm not sure that's a good idea yet."

"Huh?"

Annie glanced at Ian and then at Peter. "All this time, I've been looking for information about you, I've been working under the premise that you had been killed back in 1943. I didn't really expect to find you just a few miles away."

"I don't understand."

"Well, her son, Carl, got a little defensive about me talking to her about you. I think he's worried it might upset his mother. I think I'd better talk things over with him before we actually let Lilly know you're alive."

"Lilly's not—" Peter's expression was a little uneasy. "She's all right, isn't she? I mean, she's able to take care of her own affairs and everything, right?"

"Oh, yes," Annie assured him. "She's really doing fine."

Peter lifted his chin. "Then I'm not sure why she can't see whomever she wants to see."

"I know what you mean, and I agree with you one-hundred percent. But her son is pretty protective of her." Annie grinned. "You should understand. She says you were pretty protective of her too."

"Guilty as charged, I guess." His grin faded. "But after all this time, I just can't—"

She squeezed his hand again. "Just be patient a little longer. I will talk to Carl; maybe he'll change his mind. We'll figure something out."

He nodded and then smiled again. "I'm glad to hear she's doing so well."

"And there's that new great-great-grandbaby of hers."

There was a touch of wistfulness in his smile. "Yeah. It doesn't seem possible, but I guess it has been that long. I tell you what, that's a little one I'd love to see."

Annie paused for a moment. Surely it wouldn't hurt anything.

"You know, I practically promised I'd go see the baby," she said. "Newborns are so adorable. How would you like to come with me?"

— 13 —

"Go with you?"

Peter looked startled. So did Ian.

"We wouldn't need to do anything but take a quick look in at the nursery," Annie assured them.

"Oh, no." Peter shook his head. "If her family would rather I didn't—"

"They don't have to know anything about it. There's no reason anyone can't go see the babies. Lots of people do. No one has to know which particular baby you're looking at."

"I don't know, Annie. It just doesn't seem ...."

"You aren't busy right now, are you?"

"I can't just leave now," he protested. "I have company."

She giggled, seeing he was weakening. "You know you want to."

"But—"

"It'll take just a few minutes. We can drive you."

Ian glanced at his watch. "Actually, Annie, I have to get back pretty soon. I have a meeting."

Annie's face fell. "That's too bad. I thought Peter would enjoy going. How often do you get out anyway?"

Peter wagged a finger at her. "I'll have you know, young lady, that I still walk the half-mile to the park down the street at least once a week when the weather's good. I'm not fast, but I get there and back."

She stood up. "Well, maybe someday, though I expect if we don't go today we won't be able to see the baby at all. They send them home so quickly these days."

Peter gave her a reluctant grin. "I would like to see Lilly's great-great-grandbaby. I still can't quite imagine it's been long enough for it to be that many greats, but I guess time sneaks up on us when we're not looking. And I suppose I won't get another chance to see this little one, will I?"

"Probably not," Annie said with a sigh.

"All right, then, let's go."

"But Ian has to—"

Peter shook his head. "I'll drive us."

. *   *   *   *

Peter drove an old Lincoln Town Car, dark blue and meticulously kept. He insisted on opening the passenger door for her and then closing it again once she was inside. When they got to the hospital, he again shook a finger at her.

"Now you just stay right there, Annie." He got out of the car, and with the help of his cane, walked around to open her door.

"Thank you, sir." She smiled and took his hand, trying not to actually lean on him as she got out. "I don't get treated that way very often these days. Not since my husband passed away." She grinned a little. "Well, and then there's Ian, of course."

He made a slight bow. "I may have forgotten a lot of things since the war, but I still remember my manners."

They made their way through the hospital lobby and up to the window that separated the newborns from their observers. Annie quicky scanned the names affixed to each of the occupied cribs.

"That one."

She pointed out the third crib from the left. A tiny pink little girl with a rosebud mouth, and arms and legs curled in on herself lay there under a soft blanket sound asleep. Peter squinted.

"Which one?"

"Lilly told me the last name is Wilkes. She's the one almost at the end of the row."

"Ah, I see her now." His face softened as he looked at the baby. "A great-great-grandchild. Now that's something."

"Isn't it?" Annie smiled up at him. "Not even a day old."

He didn't say anything to that. He only stared at the baby, not really seeing her, perhaps seeing something old and long ago passed or something that never was.

"Might have been mine," he murmured.

Then he caught sight of a reflection in the window and turned to look.

"Lilly." He shook his head, a rueful touch of a smile on his lips. "No, of course not."

Annie turned too. There was a young woman in the corridor now. She was dressed in a robe and slippers, and clung to the arm of a tall young man. Annie could tell Peter was trying not to stare at the girl, but there was something familiar about her. With that combination of fair hair and doe-brown eyes, she definitely brought to mind a young Lilly Pryce.

Giving Annie and Peter shy grins, the young couple stopped at the window and looked in at the babies, and most particularly, at the one in the third crib from the left.

"There she is," the young man said, his eyes glowing with loving pride as he hugged his young wife. "There's my sweetie bear."

The girl snuggled against him, radiating happiness. "She *is* perfect, isn't she?"

"Of course she is," he assured her. "She was bound to be."

They talked softly to each other for a minute or two. Annie smiled her congratulations, and Peter was silent. He only took a furtive glance or two at the girl and spent the rest of the time staring at the window, likely seeing nothing.

"Come on, honey," the new father said at last. "You ought to get your rest now. It'll be feeding time again before you know it."

In another moment, they were gone, and Annie looked questioningly at Peter.

"That's her great-granddaughter, isn't it?" He looked down the hallway where he'd seen the girl go. "Lilly's."

Annie nodded. "I'm sure she was. There's such a resemblance, isn't there?"

He smiled slightly, again that faraway look in his eyes. "Lil wasn't even as old as that the last time I saw her. I can hardly believe she and I were ever like that. Those two, the new mom and dad, they're awfully young, aren't they?"

"They're sweet." Annie took his arm. "Are you sorry you came?"

"No." He patted her hand, his smile turning warmer. "No, ma'am, not at all. I'm glad you got a chance to get a little glimpse of what Lilly was like when I last saw her. That's pretty much how I remember her too. And I'm glad I got to see the little one. I would've hated for Lilly to miss out on her kids and grandkids and all the rest of it just because I didn't come back when I thought I would. It would've been a crying shame, don't you think?"

Annie squeezed his arm. "No wonder she was crazy about you."

He laughed. "She'd tell you, too, how stubborn and overprotective I am."

"She already has."

He laughed again. "Really? I'm glad you talked me into coming. I'm glad Lilly's had such a happy life, and I'm glad I could get a little glimpse of it myself. Thank you."

Annie sighed. "I just wish she—"

"Annie?"

They both turned to see Carl Bergstrom coming down the hall.

Annie glanced at Peter and then smiled. "Carl. I wasn't expecting to see you here, though I suppose I should have."

"I thought that was you." Carl grinned through the nursery window. "In all your life, did you ever see anything cuter than that?"

"She's darling," Annie agreed, and he shook the hand she offered.

"Nice of you to come visit."

"I told your mother I would."

Carl gave Peter a polite nod and again offered his hand. "Carl Bergstrom."

Peter gave it a firm shake. "Peter Lambert. Nice to meet you."

Carl's friendly smile vanished. "You're Peter Lambert? You're *alive*?"

"I am." Peter searched the younger man's face, no doubt looking for Lilly and Jimmy in his features. "You're Lil's boy."

"Yeah." Carl shot Annie a hard look. "I thought we agreed that you weren't going to stir up all this old stuff with Mom."

"We're not stirring up anything," she told him. "I told your mother I'd come see the baby, and I talked Peter into coming with me. We didn't expect to see you or any of your family except your new great-granddaughter."

"You didn't tell Mom about him, did you?"

Annie shook her head, and his expression was suddenly not so stern.

"I'm sorry, Mr. Lambert. I don't mean to be a jerk about all this, but I can't let you hurt my mother. She's happy the way she is. She thinks you've been dead since the forties. If you suddenly pop up now, I don't know how she might take it. It would have to be a pretty bad shock, if nothing else."

Peter nodded. "I understand that, Carl. May I call you Carl? For me, 'Mr. Bergstrom' will always be your grandfather—the nice man who drove your father and me to hockey practice when the weather was bad."

"Yeah, OK."

"I don't guess your mother ever told you about me. I don't know why she would. But when we were both just kids, I promised I'd come back to her. I promised. I'd like to keep that promise. You can understand that, can't you?"

Carl crossed his arms and nodded slightly.

"I don't want anything from her," Peter said. "I just—"

"Why didn't you come back?" Carl demanded. "If you

loved her, why didn't you come home when the war was over? What happened?"

"I was in an explosion in the war. I didn't even know who I was for the longest time. Then, when my memory came back, I was stuck in East Germany until the Berlin Wall came down. When I finally did get back to the States, I looked for her. I looked for a long time, but I couldn't find her. Her parents were dead, the house had been sold, and there was no record of her anywhere. Everybody who would have known her was gone by then too." He nodded toward Annie. "She said your mother and father lived overseas most of those years."

"I guess that *would* make her a little hard to find." Carl shuffled his feet, looking away. "That's pretty hard luck for you. I know my mother. If she had had even a sliver of hope that you were still alive, she would've waited. She didn't know."

"I know that. Believe me, son, I—"

"I'm not your son!" Carl's eyes flashed. "My father loved her. He loved her better than anything, and you have no right to come in here and try to take his place. He—"

"Whoa! Whoa!" Peter held up one hand. "I'm not trying to take anyone's place. You ask your mother what I told her before I shipped out. I told her if I didn't come back, I wanted her to get married and have a family and all those things she wanted. I knew your father. He was a good man. I'd never say anything different."

Carl took a deep breath. "I'm sorry. That was … uncalled for. Really, Mr. Lambert, I understand where you're coming from. But you have to understand. Mom thinks you're dead.

She's thought that for a long time. She's OK with that. She was happy with my dad, and she's had a really good life. I'd like you to leave it at that."

Peter pressed his lips together, not saying anything for the longest time. Then he smiled slightly.

"I only want what's best for your mother. I wish you'd let her make up her own mind about whether or not she wants to see me."

"I just—" Carl shook his head. "I just don't think that's a good idea. Please."

"Carl, who's this?"

Annie turned to see a tall, angular woman coming down the corridor. She looked to be about sixty and wore a stylish if rather severe black jacket over black slacks.

"This is Annie Dawson." Carl's smile was almost apologetic as he made the introduction. "She's the one who came to visit Mom the other day. Annie, this is my wife, Marsha."

"Hi, Marsha." Annie smiled. "We just stopped by to see the baby. You must be very proud and excited."

For the first time, the woman's face softened. "She's a little angel. Of course, her parents are no more than babies themselves. I'm not sure they're ready for so much responsibility."

"Sure they are, Marsh." Carl put an arm around his wife, beaming through the glass at the baby. "We weren't even as old as they are when we had our first."

"Well, back in our day, people grew up a lot faster." Marsha crossed her arms. "Callie and Max won't have a clue about what to do with that little girl."

"I'm sure they will," Carl said with a chuckle, "and if they don't, I'm sure you'll tell them."

Marsha only lifted one carefully plucked eyebrow at him and then glanced at Peter.

"Is this your father?" she asked Annie, and Annie smiled.

"No, just a friend."

"Peter Lambert, ma'am," Peter said, offering her his hand.

After a moment Marsha gave it a perfunctory shake. "Do you know my mother-in-law too?"

"I did a very long time ago," Peter told her. "But she's likely forgotten all about me by now. I just came along with Annie to see the baby."

"Peter Lambert." Marsha looked at him for a moment, obviously trying to remember something. "Has your mother mentioned a Peter Lambert to us before, Carl?"

"I don't think so, but like the man says, it's been a long time. Mom's probably forgotten all that by now."

"I suppose," she said finally. "Well, we ought to be going now if we're going to pick up those things Callie asked for."

"Yeah, I suppose we should." Carl smiled at Annie and Peter. "Thanks for coming to see the baby. We're pretty stuck on her."

"You ought to be," Annie said, returning the smile.

"It's really been good to meet you, Carl." Peter shook his hand again. "I hope we'll run into each other again sometime."

"Guess you never know," Carl replied, and then the uncertain look on his face was replaced by a hint of a grin. "I'm glad you got to see the baby though. Not that I'm biased or anything, but she's worth the price of admission all by herself."

Annie laughed. "She is that."

Once the Bergstroms were gone, Annie took Peter's arm and turned him toward the exit.

"Is he anything like his father?"

Peter nodded. "He's got Lilly's eyes, but he's built like Jimmy, stocky and strong. I just wish he didn't object to me seeing Lilly. I don't know what he thinks that would hurt."

Annie squeezed his arm as they walked. "Maybe, once he's had a chance to think things through, he'll change his mind. I mean, it *would* be quite a shock for her to know you're alive after so long."

"I suppose it would be." There was pleading in Peter's smile. "But I've been waiting seventy years to see her. It just doesn't seem right not to finally get to do it."

"No, I don't think so either. But give him a little time. He seems like a nice man. I bet he'll come around before long."

He gave her a wry grin. "I don't think that wife of his cared for me much though."

"She did kind of look like she suspected you of something." Annie raised one eyebrow and pretended to be suspicious. "What exactly have you been up to?"

He laughed and led her out into the afternoon sun.

*   *   *   *

Over the next few days, Annie and the other members of the Hook and Needle Club were busy planning the Easter banquet, finalizing the menu and divvying up the myriad of tasks that would be required to make the event a success. One of Annie's duties was to return to the two assisted-living facilities and get a final head count for any of their residents who would be attending the church service and the banquet and find out which, if any, would prefer to come to the banquet only.

Once she had finished her talk with Mrs. Rigsby, Annie decided to stop by and visit with Lilly. She was dying to tell her about Peter, but of course, she wouldn't be able to. Not yet. But at least she could spend a little time with her. Maybe if she and Lilly really got to be friends, her son would see that she had only Lilly's best interests at heart.

She tapped on the door to Lilly's apartment.

"Come in."

Annie smiled at Lilly's sweet voice and opened the door. "Hi, Lilly. I hope you don't mind me dropping by."

Lilly beamed at her. "Not at all, Annie. Come in.

"I was just over at Seaside Hills making the last of the arrangements for people to be able to come to the Easter banquet. I thought while I was out and about, I'd come see how you were doing and see if I can put you on our list of definites."

"Oh, yes! I'd love it. I don't get to church as often as I should. Carl takes me sometimes, but his wife is so busy taking care of her aunt at their house, he likes to give her a break on Sundays." Lilly smiled. "I guess it's hard trying to balance everyone's needs in a family."

Annie sat down on the couch beside her. "I was always lucky. My in-laws were really wonderful. They even got to be great friends with my parents. It made it so nice for all of us."

"That makes me wonder what it might have been like if

I had married Peter." There was a twinkle in the big brown eyes. "I guess I would have had to learn some German pretty quickly."

Annie bit her lip, remembering what Carl had said about his mother being deeply upset by their earlier discussion of the war and Peter. Maybe she should turn the conversation in another direction. But Lilly didn't seem upset now. She seemed calm and happy. Annie just had to ask her, especially since Lilly had been the one to bring up the subject.

"Lilly, will you tell me something honestly?"

Lilly blinked, still smiling faintly. "If I can."

"The last time we talked, Carl called me and said that you were very upset and crying afterward."

"Oh, poppycock! I get a little sentimental over the past sometimes, but that makes it sound like I was prostrate with grief, which I certainly was not."

Annie wrinkled her brow. "Why would he say that? Why would he want us not to talk about Peter and the diary and everything? Did he say?"

Lilly only looked heavenward. "Bless him. Ever since Jimmy died, and I moved back to the States, Carl thinks I'm too fragile for even the slightest upset. He didn't really say much to me, just that I shouldn't be dwelling on the past and all. I'm so sorry he bothered you."

Annie smiled, relieved. "Oh, it was no bother. I'm just glad you weren't truly upset. I promised him I wouldn't bring up Peter anymore."

Lilly sighed. "Oh, I'm sorry. I've really enjoyed—"

"I didn't promise I wouldn't talk to you about him if you brought it up."

The two of them shared a conspiratorial grin

"Not that we can't talk about other things too, you know," Annie said, looking around the room at the amazing works of needle art that hung on the walls. "I belong to a needlework club that meets every week at A Stitch in Time downtown. Have you been there?"

"Oh, yes." Lilly's expression was blissful. "A stitcher's paradise. I just wish I hadn't had to give up sewing. If I hadn't, I think I'd be over there all the time—so many beautiful threads and patterns."

"You know," Annie said, her eyes twinkling, "if you ever feel up to it, and if you wouldn't mind, of course, I know everyone in our club would love to see your beautiful work."

Lilly flushed with pleasure. "Oh, do you think so? I'd love to have them come by. It would be like a party."

"We wouldn't want to be any trouble, and we wouldn't have to stay long. But I know they'd love all this. It takes a needlecrafter to really appreciate the hours and hours of work that go into projects like these." Annie patted Lilly's soft hand. "Anyway, just something to think about when you're feeling up to it one day. I know you'd be a big hit with all the ladies. They were positively green with envy when Alice and I told them about all this when we were here last time."

"Oh, you're too sweet. Would you like some coffee? I was about to make myself some."

Lilly stood up and then dropped heavily onto the couch again, blinking rapidly as her breathing sped up.

"Lilly, are you all right?" Annie went to her, taking her trembling hand. "Are you OK?"

"Having a little ... trouble ... breathing," Lilly gasped out. She managed a small smile, but the fear in her eyes was much more genuine. "I'll be ... all right."

"Do you want me to call someone?"

"No, no. It comes and goes." Lilly took several more quick breaths. "I'm fine. I'm ..."

"I'm going call 911."

Lilly shook her head, still gasping. "No ... I don't need—"

"Lilly, please. Just to make sure."

Lilly clutched the arm of the couch, her breath coming a little more rapidly now. Finally, she closed her eyes and nodded her head. Annie grabbed her cellphone.

— 14 —

A few minutes later, two paramedics were at Lilly's door. One was a sturdy-looking young woman with auburn hair tied in a thick braid down her back. The other was a rather lanky young man with a mop of black hair.

"How are you doing, ma'am?" he asked Lilly when Annie ushered him in to see her, and his voice was carefully distinct. "Are you having trouble breathing?"

Lilly nodded, looking more frightened than before when he took an oxygen mask from his partner and strapped it over Lilly's mouth and nose.

"Now you just breathe deep, ma'am, and try to relax while we see what's going on here."

The two paramedics checked Lilly's vital signs and asked her a number of questions. Then they brought in a gurney.

"We're going to take you to the hospital now, ma'am," the young man told her. "Just to have you checked out. OK?"

Lilly shook her head. "No, really, I feel fine now. I don't need to go."

"Ma'am, we don't know what's wrong with you, but the hospital will be able to run some tests and make sure this doesn't happen again. OK?"

"Really, I feel fine."

She looked at Annie and so did the paramedic.

"Are you family, ma'am?" he asked.

Annie shook her head. "Just a friend."

"We'd really like her to go get checked out. We can't make her go if she doesn't want to, but it would be the best thing. Maybe you could convince her?"

Annie knelt down beside the couch.

"Oh, Annie." Lilly reached a hand out to her, and Annie hurried to take it, reading the distress on the older woman's face.

"They just want to take you to the hospital. I don't think it's anything bad, but you really ought to find out for certain. Better for them to be too careful than not careful enough, right?"

"But, really, Annie, I feel fine now. It was just a little spell. They didn't say anything is wrong with me, did they?"

"You know how it is," Annie said, patting her hand. "They like to check everything a hundred different ways, just to be sure. And they never tell anyone anything until they're all done."

Lilly's grip tightened. "You don't suppose something's really the matter, and they just don't want to say anything, do you?"

"I don't know." Annie stood up, still holding her hand. "You should go to the hospital now and let them see what they can find out. If you're already feeling better, it's probably not much of anything. But it's better to know for sure—right?"

"But Carl—"

"I can call Carl for you once we're on our way. He can meet us at the hospital. You know he's going to be upset with you if you don't take care of yourself."

"You don't mind calling him?"

"Not at all. Not as long as I can tell him you're being taken care of. What do you think?"

"Oh, would you?" Lilly gave her a small, uncertain smile from behind her oxygen mask. "I would really appreciate it."

"Now, let's get you taken care of, and then I'll call him. Please don't worry. I'm sure you're in good hands." Annie smiled at the two paramedics. "You'll take very good care of her, won't you?"

"Yes, ma'am," the young woman assured her.

Lilly looked at Annie, dark eyes pleading. "Would you come with me? I'd feel so much better about going if you would."

"I don't know if I can." Annie turned to one of the paramedics. "Is it OK if I ride with her?"

"As long as it's all right with the patient," the young man said.

"Oh, yes, please."

Lilly nodded earnestly, and the two of them helped Lilly to her feet and then settled her on the gurney.

"Do you have a purse with your keys in it?" Annie asked before they could wheel Lilly away.

Again, Lilly nodded. "On my night table in the bedroom."

Annie scooped up the little black handbag, and once everyone was outside, locked up behind her. As soon as the ambulance was underway, she got Lilly to tell her Carl's phone number. His phone rang four times and then finally clicked over to his voice mail.

This is Carl. Leave me a message.

"Hello, Carl? This is Annie Dawson. I don't want you to

worry, but I was visiting your mother a little while ago, and she had some trouble breathing. We're on our way to the hospital right now, and I thought you'd want to meet us there."

Lilly reached over for Annie's hand. "Tell him not to worry," she whispered. "I'm fine." Annie nodded, smiling at her. "She's doing very well right now and doesn't want you to worry. They're taking good care of her. I hope you get this message soon. Please call me when you do." She gave her phone number twice and then hung up.

"I got his voice mail, but don't worry. I'm sure he'll call right back."

Her phone rang, and she smiled at Lilly. "I bet that's him. Hello?"

"Annie? This is Carl Bergstrom. I didn't recognize your number or I would have picked up. What's going on with Mom?"

"We're on our way to the hospital right now, as I told you. She's doing fine. Can you meet us there?"

"Sure. I'm over in Newcastle on business, but I'm headed your way. I'll be there as soon as I can."

"I'll be waiting for you."

They were soon at the hospital, and Lilly was wheeled away. Annie sat down in the beige-bland waiting room, hoping to catch Carl when he came in. Minutes later, her phone rang again.

"Carl?"

"Annie? It's Peter Lambert."

"Peter! How did you know?"

He didn't say anything for a second. "How did I know what?"

Of course he couldn't know what was going on with Lilly. She took a deep breath. "I'm sorry. I'm a little tied up right now. What's up?"

"I was just calling to see if you had a chance to talk to Carl, but if you're busy, we can talk later."

"I haven't talked to him about you seeing Lilly, Peter. I will, I promise. When I get the right opportunity. I—"

Dr. Howard to ICU, stat. The loudspeaker blared, cutting Annie off, and she heard Peter take a breath.

"Where are you? Is everything all right?"

Annie cringed. "I don't want you worrying, Peter, but I'm up at the hospital with Lilly."

"What?"

"She's all right. She just had some trouble breathing, and they brought her in to the hospital."

There was only silence on the other end of the line.

"Peter?"

"She's not—"

"I'm sorry, but I really don't know much. She was feeling breathless and weak, and they thought she should be checked out. It doesn't sound like anything too serious, but I'm waiting to see what they say. Her son is on the way here too."

"I'll meet you there."

"Peter, you're not supposed to …."

She broke off when she heard a click. With a sigh, she put her phone back into her purse and picked up a magazine, prepared to wait.

* * * *

True to his word, Peter came into the waiting room a few minutes later.

"How is she?" he asked, hurrying to her as fast as his bad knee would allow.

"I haven't heard anything yet. I'm sure they wouldn't tell me anything anyway since I'm not family."

"OK. But I want to know what you find out, if you find out anything. I ... I want to be here, even if I can't see her."

She slipped her arm into his, squeezing it a little. "I'm sorry this all hasn't worked out the way you wanted. The way we both wanted. But maybe, if you'll just be patient for a while ...."

He smiled a little wryly. "After seventy years, I don't know if I have time to be patient anymore. If something happens to her now, and I never got to see her. After I was so close." He shook his head and didn't say anything for a few seconds. "What happened?"

"I already told you what I know," Annie said. "We were talking, and she suddenly had trouble breathing. When the ambulance got there, the EMTs gave her some oxygen and she felt a lot better, but we convinced her to come and get checked out. Just to be sure."

"I'm glad you were with her, and I'm glad you got her to come to the hospital." He took a deep breath and then let it out in a whoosh.

Annie looked into his worried eyes, waiting for him to go on.

"After all these years," he said. "I'm afraid I'm not going to get to see her at all."

Before she could answer, Carl hurried into the waiting room. He went straight to the nurse's station and spoke to the woman on duty. After she did some checking, she pointed him back toward the waiting area.

"Carl." Annie stood up as he came toward her. "You made good time."

"I guess they didn't tell you anything either?"

"No." She took his arm. "Come sit down. It may be a while."

Carl's eyes widened when he saw Peter sitting there, and then he frowned.

"What are *you* doing here?"

"I wanted to find out how your mother is doing," Peter said evenly. "Same as you."

Carl glared at him and then turned icy eyes back to Annie. "I thought we agreed it was best if he didn't see her. If she didn't even know about him."

"I didn't come to see her." Peter said. "I wanted to talk to you."

Carl narrowed his eyes. "What about?"

Peter nodded toward the chair next to him. "Would you care to sit?"

"All right."

He sat down, and for a moment no one said anything. Then Peter put his hand gently on Carl's arm.

"First, please, understand that I would never do anything to harm your mother."

"What happened?" Carl asked, his face stern.

"I was just at her apartment," Annie said. "We were just talking when she suddenly couldn't breathe."

"What were you talking about?" Carl demanded, and he jerked his chin toward Peter. "Him? Was he there too?"

"No." Annie forced her voice to stay calm and low. "It was just your mother and me. I came to talk to her about the Easter banquet we're having at Stony Point. We chatted about a few things. I told her I thought my needlework club would like to see some of the cross-stitch pieces she's done."

Carl's face relaxed a bit. "Yeah, she hated having to give that up."

"She made some really beautiful things," Annie said. "It's too bad she had to quit. That must have given her a lot of pleasure."

"Yeah. Gave her something to do after Dad passed on. I just—"

"Mrs. Bergstrom's family?"

Carl stood up as the doctor approached. "I'm her son."

The young doctor shook Carl's hand. "I'm Doctor Parker. If you'll come with me, I'll get you up to speed on your mother's condition."

The two men disappeared through some swinging doors, leaving Peter and Annie to watch anxiously after them.

"I guess we wait again," Peter said.

"Maybe it won't be too long."

Annie gave him a hopeful smile. It was just a few minutes later when Carl came back into the waiting room.

"How is she?" Annie asked him.

Carl sighed wearily. "A lot better, they say. They haven't actually found anything wrong, but they've been keeping her on oxygen." He grinned slightly. "Of course, she's already kicking to get out of here."

A little of the anxiousness in Peter's eyes lifted. "That's good to hear. If she's fussing to get out, it can't be that bad."

"Yeah, that's what I thought." Carl gave him a reluctant smile. "Anyway, they're making sure there's nothing else they ought to check out. She'll probably go home tomorrow or the next day."

"Oh, thank God," Annie said. "That's good news."

"Yeah." Carl looked at Peter again. "So ... that's really all there is to know. I'll let Annie know if there are any complications or anything. Umm ... thanks for coming and everything."

"I was happy to," Peter said, "but I'd still like to have a word with you, if I may."

"I know you mean well, Mr. Lambert," Carl said, glancing toward the door, "but I really don't think now is a good time."

Peter frowned. "I know you want to look after your mother. And I don't blame you, especially if you promised your father. But I made a promise too, and I'm not any different from you about being a man of my word."

Carl shook his head. "I can't let you get back in touch with her. I can't let her know you're alive. I can't let you tell her about my dad. She has good memories of him. They had a good marriage, and I can't let you ruin that just so you can play the long-lost hero."

Peter glanced at Annie and then looked back at Carl. "I'm afraid I don't understand. How would—"

Looking over his shoulder, Carl again shook his head. "Look, it really doesn't matter if you understand. For my mother's sake, this is how it's got to be. And I'd really appreciate it if you wouldn't bring this up in front of my wife."

Annie looked up to see Marsha Bergstrom coming into the waiting room, her smile thin.

"Hello," Marsha said. "I'm surprised to see you both again. How'd you know Lilly was here?"

"I went to see her at her apartment," Annie said. "When she started having trouble, I called the ambulance and rode over to the hospital with her. Peter just wanted to see how she was doing."

"Well, you know how it is with older people." Marsha glanced at Peter. "Things can hit them all of a sudden."

Annie kept her expression pleasant. "It's good to know that they haven't found anything really wrong with her and that she should be able to go home soon."

"Yes, it is." Marsha looked at Annie, eyes narrowed and then turned to her husband. "Have they let you see her yet, Carl?"

"No, not yet. The doctor said they'd call me when we could come back where she is. Shouldn't be long now. I was telling Mr. Lambert here that they probably won't let her have any other visitors for a while though. But we'll make sure and let him know how she's doing in the next day or so."

Marsha turned to Peter. "I'm sorry you came all the way here for nothing, Mr. Lambert."

Peter smiled slightly. "Well, like I told you before, Lilly and I were old friends before the war, and I thought I'd like to look her up again. Just for old times' sake. But I'm thinking now might not be the best time."

"Old friends?" Again Marsha narrowed her eyes.

Peter grinned. "Very old. But maybe she doesn't need

somebody like me stopping by when she's not feeling well. I just wanted to see for myself that she was doing all right."

"It was nice of him, Marsh, don't you think?" Carl said. "But he's right. Now's probably not the best time to be renewing old acquaintances."

Marsha put one hand on her hip. "What triggered this spell of hers anyway? Maybe she shouldn't have so many visitors. It can't be good for her to get overexcited."

"I don't think she was overexcited," Annie said. "We were just talking about my grandmother and about cross-stitch. They both were real artists with their threads."

Marsha rolled her eyes. "Well that's certainly not going to make anyone overexcited."

"We were just having a nice conversation," Annie added, making sure to keep her expression pleasant. "I really don't know what could have triggered the episode."

"I still wonder if it's wise for her to have so many visitors." Marsha repeated, pursing her lips. "Just a waste of good money on all this emergency care, when all of this could have been prevented with just a little common sense."

Annie and Peter exchanged an incredulous glance, and Carl looked down at the carpet.

"Come on, Marsha," he said. "She's got good insurance for what Medicare doesn't cover. Besides, it's just money."

Marsha looked at Annie. "Don't get me wrong. I want her to get whatever care she needs, of course. But it seems like she doesn't actually have anything wrong with her, and this is going to end up being a pretty expensive checkup."

Annie still managed to smile. "Well, it'll be worth it to know she's really all right. Besides, whatever this visit costs,

it has to be less expensive than if they find something seriously wrong, don't you think?"

"Yes, I suppose so," Marsha said. "Well, thank you for
making sure she was taken care of, Mrs. Dawson." She nodded curtly at Peter. "Thank you for coming to check on her.
We'll be fine now. Carl and I can see to everything from here
on out."

They were definitely being dismissed.

"Ready to go, Annie?" Peter asked evenly.

Annie nodded, taking the arm he offered, and then she
handed Lilly's purse to Marsha. "She wanted me to grab
that for her and lock up on our way out."

"I'll see that she gets it." Marsha tucked the purse
under her arm. "Thanks."

"I appreciate your concern," Carl said, his tone apologetic. "Both of you."

He shook Peter's hand.

"Take care of her, Carl." Peter smiled slightly and then
gave Marsha a grave nod. "Mrs. Bergstrom."

Annie glared back toward the waiting room once they
were out in the parking lot. "That Marsha makes me so
mad. She acts like Lilly is spending *their* money instead of
her own."

Peter shrugged. "I'm afraid, when their parents get older, a lot of people start making plans about what they'll do
with what they have coming in inheritance. They start feeling deprived if they don't think they're going to get every
last penny."

"What was Lilly supposed to do? Nothing?"

Peter opened the car door for her. "I don't think Marsha

expected her to do nothing. Maybe she just thinks she was … overcautious.'"

Scowling, Annie got into the car and buckled herself in. "Well, Marsha wasn't there at the time. It was scary seeing Lilly struggling to breathe. Besides, Lilly didn't want to go to the hospital. I had to convince her, and I'm glad I did. It's not worth taking a chance with things like that."

Peter got into the driver's seat and smiled at her. "Thanks for caring about Lilly. You know, I continue to be amazed at how many people have looked after her all these years." His smile turned a little rueful. "I always thought that was going to be *my* job."

She patted his hand. "Maybe it still can be."

He frowned. "Not if Carl has anything to say about it." They were silent for a moment. "You're a good friend, Annie. Even if you haven't known Lilly long, I can already see that you're looking out for her. Thank you for doing that, especially since I can't. At least not yet."

She smiled at him. "Lilly's a sweetheart, and I'm happy to do whatever I can for her—and for you. You're a pretty good friend too. Thanks for taking me back to my car."

"It's no trouble at all. Happy to do it. Where are we going?"

"Back to Lilly's. Oh, I guess you don't know where that is."

"Nope." Again he chuckled. "That seems to be a closely guarded secret."

"I'm sorry. This is all so silly, you know? I mean, I don't understand why Carl is so uneasy about you seeing his mother again."

"You know I could just look her up in the phone book if I really wanted to now, right?"

Annie giggled. "You sure could. OK, head back to the highway. Lilly's place isn't far."

"He looks a lot like Jimmy, you know?" Peter pulled out into the street, his expression thoughtful. "But I can see Lilly in him too. Especially in the eyes, don't you think?"

Annie smiled. "I can see that. He certainly takes good care of her too."

"Yeah, I like that about him. Once I remembered everything, I always worried that she was alone or in trouble somewhere. I'm glad she had a family to look after her." Peter thought for a moment. "I just don't get what he was saying about Jimmy? What does he think I would tell her about his dad?"

"I don't know."

He laughed abruptly. "If it's something that would upset Lilly, then I don't know what it would be. Truth be told, I can't think of a single thing."

~ 15 ~

Four days and interminable rounds of inconclusive tests later, Lilly was sent home from the hospital with a bottle of oxygen, just in case she needed it. Her son had also insisted she either agree to wear a medical alert bracelet or go back to live permanently at Seaside Hills Assisted Living. Lilly chose the bracelet.

The following Tuesday, at the next Hook and Needle Club meeting, Annie brought her friends up to speed on the Lilly-and-Peter saga.

"You mean Peter and Lilly have been living within just a few miles of each other all of this time?" Peggy asked.

"Yes," Annie said. "It almost sounds like a fairy tale, but Lilly doesn't even know her Prince Charming is still alive."

"You're not going to tell her?" Alice said. "I think she deserves to know. Why is Lilly's son so dead-set against it?"

"That is the oddest part of this. When Peter and I were at the hospital waiting for word about Lilly, Carl was adamant that Lilly should know *nothing* about Peter. Carl wouldn't talk to Peter about it ... wouldn't budge an inch."

"Just because Lilly is elderly doesn't mean she's incapable of making a decision on her own," said Stella. "I would be apoplectic if someone tried to make a decision like that for me."

"I would too, Stella," Annie said. "I'm going by to check

on Lilly after the meeting. Now that I've discovered the answer to the mystery behind Lilly and Peter, I think I'm going to stick around until I can figure out why Carl thinks his mother's old beau is such a threat to her health."

*   *   *   *

After the meeting, Annie dropped by Lilly's apartment, making sure she had what she needed and that she wasn't having any more difficulties with her breathing. Since Lilly's hospital stay, Annie had looked in on Lilly a couple of times. Once she found Carl already there, just leaving as Annie arrived. Their passing was, at best, set in chilly silence.

A week later, Annie again went to check on Lilly after the Hook and Needle Club meeting. As she left, Annie met Carl walking up to his mother's apartment and stopped him before he could go in.

"May we talk for just a moment?"

He looked at her warily. "Do we have anything to talk about?"

"I think you know."

He shook his head. "We're done with that, aren't we? I thought we'd agreed you wouldn't bring the whole Peter Lambert thing up with Mom."

"We did. But that doesn't mean she hasn't brought it up with me. When I first met her, I told her I was going to find out what happened to him. Now she wants to know what I've found. What am I supposed to tell her?"

"Tell her you ran into a dead end and couldn't find out anything else. How hard is that?"

"It's not true, Carl." Annie pressed her lips together, trying not to lose her temper. "And it's not fair. She wants to know. Peter wants to see her. Do you have any idea how much he's wanted to see her for the past seventy years? How can you refuse him?"

"He'll just have to get over it." Carl narrowed his eyes at her. "He knows Mom is all right. He knows she's safe and taken care of. Isn't that enough?"

"Not for Peter. And not for your mother."

"Look, the last time you talked to her about him, she cried all day."

"That's not true, Carl, and you know it. I asked her about that. She said she was fine then."

"Well, talking about him was enough to put her into the hospital."

Annie pursed her lips. "Now you're just being silly. I told you, we were talking about my grandmother and about sewing that day. Nothing about Peter or the war or anything like that. What is it really? Why don't you want her to talk to Peter?"

He shook his head. "We really don't need to be standing out on the street talking about family business, do we?"

"Please, Carl." She reached her hand out to him. "Help me understand. Why can't your mother know Peter is alive and still wanting to see her? I don't want to do anything that would hurt her. I know Peter doesn't. As Peter told me, you know that now he could just look her up in the phone book and call her. But he hasn't. Have you thought about that? He hasn't because he is trying to do the right thing. In fairness to him, can't you just tell us why it would be bad for her?"

For a long moment, he only looked at her, jaws and fists clenched. Then he exhaled heavily.

"You know Moody's Diner out on Route 1 in Waldoboro?"

She nodded. "Haven't been there, but I've heard they have great pie."

He glanced at his watch. "I have to see Mom, and then there are some things I have to get done. If you and Mr. Lambert want to meet me at Moody's at four, we can talk this all out. Fair enough?"

"That works for me. I'll call Peter. If he can't meet us for some reason, I'll call you right back. OK?"

He nodded reluctantly. "I don't know why you have to rake up this old stuff, but, yeah, I guess it's best to get things straight. Then you'll see that I'm right about all this."

*   *   *   *

Moody's Diner was a low, white-painted building under a bright neon sign, a slice of Americana that had sat out on the highway for nearly ninety years.

Annie grinned at the sign that read, "Pie fixes everything," and then glanced up at the clock that hung just to the right of the red exit sign above the door. Four-fifteen.

Peter frowned. "He's not coming, is he?"

"Just give it a few more minutes. If he's not here by twenty after, I'll give him a call." Annie grinned at him. "How's your pie?"

His expression softened, and he gave her a faint smile in return. "Delicious. Apple has always been my favorite. Yours?"

"Excellent," she assured him, and she took another bite of her cheesecake. "Oh, here he is." Annie smiled and waved as Carl Bergstrom came into the diner. She slid over as he hurried up to the table, making room for him on her side of the booth.

"Sorry I'm late," he said, shaking the hand Peter offered and then sitting next to Annie. "I should have called to let you know I was running behind, but I was stuck on the phone with a client all the way here."

Annie shook her head. "It's no problem. We were enjoying the pie. Would you like some …?"

Before she could finish, the waitress brought Carl a cup of coffee and a piece of banana cream pie.

"Thanks, Jenny," he told her, and then he smirked. "Yeah, I come here once in a while."

Annie raised an eyebrow at him, and he chuckled.

"OK, once a week or so. So, sue me. I like pie."

Annie smiled and then sobered at the look that passed between Carl and Peter. Clearly, Peter wasn't willing to wait any longer for an explanation.

"I guess you agreed to talk to us for a reason," the older man said. "We're listening."

Carl sighed. "I was hoping I wouldn't have to get into this with you. I told you before that I'm not going to let you hurt my mother. She loved my dad, and I'm not going to have you spoil her memories of him. It should be obvious to you, Mr. Lambert, why I don't want you coming back into her life."

Peter glanced at Annie, no doubt wondering if she understood what Carl meant. Annie could only shrug.

He turned back to Carl. "Obvious? I don't know what

you mean by obvious. I don't know what you think I'm going to tell your mother if I talk to her. I'd never say anything against your dad, Carl. Besides being my friend, he was Lilly's husband. I respect that."

Carl looked at him, eyes narrowed. "Why wouldn't you tell her? He knew. All along, he knew, and he never told her."

"What are you talking about?" Peter frowned. "What did he know?"

"He knew you were alive."

Annie drew a breath audibly, but Peter only clenched his jaw and tightened his grip on his cane.

"How?"

Carl looked angry and apologetic all at once. "I didn't know. Not till the very last. I suppose he carried that secret all those years they were married. It wasn't until he knew he was dying that he said anything."

*   *   *   *

October, 2002

Guam's bright sunshine flooded the military hospital room. Carl peered around the half-open door to see his mother sitting in a chair beside the bed, her head leaning on one hand, her eyes closed.

"Mom?"

She looked up, startled, and then relief washed over her tired face. "Carl."

She started to get up, but he hurried over to her, embracing her where she was.

"I'm sorry I couldn't make it any sooner, Mom. How is he?" They both looked over at the silent figure on the bed, and then Carl took his dad's still hand. "How is he?"

"He seems to be failing fast." She somehow managed a faint smile. "I asked the nurses to leave the blinds open. Even if he's about to leave us, maybe he can still tell what a beautiful day it is."

"I wanted to be with him at the last," Carl said. "How long has he been out?"

"He hasn't spoken since yesterday afternoon. I would have called you sooner, if I had known the end was so close."

Carl sank into the chair on the other side of his father's bed and heaved a sigh. "I do wish I had been able to talk to him just one more time. I just couldn't make the flights work out." He rubbed his eyes before turning his attention to his mother. "How about you, Mom? You don't look like you've slept in days."

"That recliner in the corner doesn't double as a bed so well."

"Why don't you take a break and go have lunch?" Carl asked. "I can stay here with Dad."

"My friend Nancy is in the waiting area." She glanced uncertainly at the bed. "She's been great about keeping me company, and I'm sure she'd like to take a little break, too, but I hate to leave."

"I'm sure it'll be OK. You two go and have a good lunch. We'll be here when you get back."

"If you're sure, son."

His mother came over to his side of the bed, and Carl stood to embrace her. No words were needed. Then she leaned down to kiss her husband's cheek, picked up her purse and walked out of the room.

Carl sat again, and in a short time, slipped into sleep. He didn't know how long he had been asleep, probably just a few minutes, when he was startled awake.

"Lilly!"

Jimmy was trying to sit upright. Carl sprang to his feet and eased him back to the pillows.

"Mom's not here, Dad," he said gently. "She went for lunch with a friend."

"Carl?" Jimmy looked as if he wasn't sure he was seeing straight. "How long have you been here?"

"I just got in."

"And Mom's not here?"

"No, but she'll be back soon."

"I know I don't have much time, son. I need to tell you something. I need to get it off my chest. Before I go." Jimmy gripped Carl's hand like a vise, and he looked as if he were summoning the courage and strength to continue.

"Dad, you're not—"

"Just listen to me, Carl. Listen. You remember Mom and me talking about Peter Lambert?"

"Sure, I guess. But that was a long time ago, Dad. What's that matter now?"

"He and your mother had an understanding that they would get married after the war. Well, I was stationed in Berlin right after the surrender in May of 1945. It was still pure bedlam; the city was all torn up from the bombing and artillery. We were moving a bunch of civilians when, in that crowd, I saw him. I saw Peter!"

His father's grip tightened, and Carl could see how important this was to him. Maybe it didn't matter why. He just had to let his dad say what he needed to say.

"Okay, Dad."

"At least I'm pretty sure it was Peter." Dad frowned, struggling to remember. "I called out to him—called his name—but he didn't respond. It was like he never knew me. I don't know—maybe it wasn't him."

"I don't know, Dad. Maybe not."

"I knew Peter had been reported as missing in action and presumed dead," he continued, almost exhausted now. "I guess my mind was playing tricks on me. I started rationalizing, trying to convince myself it couldn't have been him." He looked up at his son, eyes desperate now. "But I *knew* it was! And I knew that, if Peter Lambert was alive, your mother would never marry me. So, God forgive me, I didn't tell anyone. I don't know what was wrong with him, but we never heard from him again. I assume he died in Berlin."

"Dad!"

"I know it was wrong, Carl. Love can make you do stupid things. Your mother and I have made a good life for ourselves, but she deserved better than me." His eyes grew moist. "She deserved Peter. I can't undo what I did, but she needs to know about this, and I need to get this right before her and God before I die. Promise me that you'll tell her if she doesn't get back here in time."

"But Dad—"

"No, Carl! Promise!"

"I'm not sure Mom would want to know, but I'll tell her."

"Thank you. I love you, son."

Dad's voice was weaker now. He whispered something else, inaudible, and then Carl watched him slip back into silence.

"I love you, too, Dad."

*   *   *   *

"When Mom got back, Dad was completely unresponsive again," Carl said. "He died without regaining consciousness." He looked up at Peter and Annie over what was left of his cup of coffee. "I know it was wrong, Mr. Lambert. He did too. That's why he wanted to get it off his chest before he died. That's why he wanted to get things straight with Mom. I know how it must look to you, but he did love her. He did."

"Evidently not enough to tell her the truth." There was more than a little bitterness in Peter's tone, and there was a long, taut moment of silence.

Carl sighed. "For all I knew, you were dead, Mr. Lambert." Carl's head bowed to his hands. "I just couldn't tell her then." He looked up at Peter. "And I don't think there's a reason for her to know now."

Awkward silence again enveloped the table, and it was a minute or more before Peter finally spoke.

"I don't think I would've told her either, Carl. As you say, there's no use spoiling her memory of your father now. Funny thing is—I couldn't have told her anyway. I didn't see him. Or if I did, I don't remember it." There was a touch of wryness in Peter's smile. "I wouldn't have known him if I had seen him. Not back then. I was in an explosion in '43. I didn't even know my own name for another twenty years."

Carl looked at him, wide-eyed. "He said he saw you. He called you by name, but he figured you didn't hear him. Then, when he got out of the Army and got back home, he found out you were believed killed. He didn't say anything. I think, after a while, he thought maybe it wasn't you after all."

"When did they get married?" Peter asked softly.

"August of 1950. It was after her parents' death. I guess she put him off for a while. And maybe Dad figured, if that was you, that you just didn't want to come back."

Peter took off his glasses, wiping the lenses and his eyes. "I guess I'm glad she wasn't alone all that time. It took me nearly fifty years to get back home. Your father gave her a home, the kids she always wanted, a good life. I couldn't begrudge her that."

"Thanks for understanding, Mr. Lambert."

"And don't worry, Carl. I'll never say anything to her about your dad. He was a good guy. Maybe he made a mistake. Maybe he thought he was doing what was best. It might not have made any difference in the long run anyway."

Carl frowned. "I can't help wondering if it might have been different for you if he'd told someone he thought he had seen you. Maybe the Army could have sent someone to check it out, compare fingerprints—something to try to bring you back."

"Then where would you be?" Peter grinned at him, and Carl laughed, half-startled. "And," Peter added, "who would've looked after your mother all these years?"

"I guess."

Carl smiled reluctantly and took a drink of his coffee. How could he not like this man? Annie was beginning to think it was impossible.

"Things happen for a reason," Peter said. "I don't pretend to understand, but I'm glad you were here to take care of Lilly. Sounds like you've been a great son, and I didn't need to worry about her at all."

"But your own life. All that time in East Berlin—I can't imagine ...."

"It was always a challenge, I'll give you that much. But I had friends. I had my work. Heck, I saw the Berlin Wall come down, firsthand. I've been a lot of places, and I've had a great life so far. The only thing that was missing was Lilly. Now that I know where she is, all that I ask is that you let her decide for herself whether or not she wants to see me. If she doesn't, I promise you I won't bother her again."

"I don't know."

"I give you my word, Carl," Peter said. "I won't tell her what you just told me. I mean about your dad and all. That's all over and done. I'd just like the chance to keep my promise. It's only right."

Carl glanced at Annie. "Would you? Do you think you might?"

She smiled. "I'll break it to her gently, I promise."

Carl looked at Peter for a long moment, eyes narrowed, and then he nodded. "All right. But whatever she decides, that's final. No trying to talk her into anything, all right?"

Annie nodded. "All right."

"Deal?"

Carl offered Peter his hand, and Peter took it.

"Deal."

The three of them talked a while longer, Carl mostly filling Peter in on his mother's life the past few years. Then he finally pushed back his empty plate.

"I guess I'd better get moving. My wife will be wondering where I am." He stood up and shook Peter's hand again. "I'm trusting you to do what's right by my mother. Don't make me sorry I did."

"I just want to keep the promise I made to her, Carl. That's all. There's no reason she has to know about what your father told you. She certainly won't hear it from me anyway."

Carl gave him a brief nod and nodded at Annie. "You be careful how you tell her."

"I will," she assured him. "Don't worry. Would you like to be there when I do?"

He thought for a second, and then he shook his head. "No. I'll leave that to you." He considered for another moment. "This is her own business, I guess. I need to let her decide what's best for herself."

He gave them both another solemn nod, and he left the diner.

Peter watched him go. "I guess I shouldn't be surprised that he's a good guy. Not if he's Lilly's boy."

Annie smiled at him. "Oh, I'm so glad he's OK with me telling her about you."

He smiled too, looking a little stunned. "I can't believe I'm going to get to see her at last."

"If it's all right with her, of course."

"Yes, of course." He nodded, staring at nothing. "She has

to. She has to see me now. After all this time, she couldn't turn me down, could she?"

His blue eyes were full of vulnerable uncertainty, and he was suddenly the boy in the photographs again, eighteen-year-old Peter leaving home and sweetheart, not knowing if he would ever come back. She reached across the table and took his hand.

"Of course not. She'll be thrilled to know you're still alive. She'll want to know everything that's happened to you since you left home all those years ago."

He smiled slightly, and then he pressed his lips together. "It might take me a little while to let go of what Jimmy did."

Annie didn't say anything. How could anyone forgive such a betrayal?

"I guess he couldn't have known about the Wall being built later on or anything like that," Peter said. "But maybe he could have told someone. Maybe they could have brought me back—helped me remember who I was. It might have saved me a whole lot of years alone. At least Lilly thought I was dead all that time. She didn't think I had just abandoned her."

"I'm sorry," Annie said finally.

He exhaled heavily and dredged up a smile. "Well, I can't build myself up by tearing him down. He's gone. Saying anything now would only hurt Lilly. I'd rather never see her again than ever do that."

She released his hand. Sitting back, she ate the last bite of her cheesecake.

"She's going to be so happy to know you're alive and that you're right here. I can still hardly believe it myself."

"Just break it to her easy. After all this time, I'm sure I'm the last person she ever expects to hear from."

"Don't you worry," Annie said, grinning at him. "I'll be careful. You'll have to be patient a while longer though. I'll give Lilly a call and see when she has time to see me. Then we'll have to go from there."

"Oh, of course. You will let me know when you hear something, won't you?"

"I promise."

As soon as they finished their coffee, Peter escorted Annie to her car. Once he had driven away, Annie grabbed her cellphone out of her purse and called Lilly's number.

"Lilly? Hi. This is Annie Dawson. I was wondering if I could stop by and see you in a few minutes."

"Annie. Hello. Is something wrong? You sound a little out of breath."

"No, no. Everything's fine. I just have something to talk to you about."

"Oh, yes?"

Annie had to keep herself from blurting out the news right that second. She'd promised Peter and Carl she would break the news to Lilly gently.

"Is it all right if I come see you right now? I'm in Waldoboro, so it will probably take me just a few minutes to get there."

"Sure."

"Great! See you in a little bit."

— 16 —

Lilly was quick to answer the door when Annie got to her
apartment. She looked up with expectation, but with
more than a hint of worry in her brown eyes.
Annie hurried to her.

"Thanks for letting me come right over. I have some
news for you, but you probably ought to sit down."

She took Lilly's arm and sat her down on the couch.

"Is everything all right?" There was a little tremor in Lilly's
voice, and she cleared her throat. "You're making me nervous."

"Don't be nervous," Annie said, urging her to sit. "Just
take a deep breath and listen. As you know, I've been doing
some research about Peter. I thought you might want to
know what I found out."

"Yes?"

"Are you sure you're prepared? It's not going to be what
you were expecting."

Lilly's dark eyes were wary. "If it's something bad, I don't
want to know." She smiled faintly. "I know I've made him a
bit of an idol over the years. I guess when you live to be only
eighteen, you don't have much time to disappoint folks."

"Lilly, it isn't that."

"No. Really. If you found out he was a coward or did
something dishonorable, I really don't want to know. I
shouldn't have had you look into all this at all."

Annie sat down on the couch and put her arm around the older woman's shoulders. "Lilly, I found him. He's still alive."

Lilly's lips trembled. "He's—"

"He's still alive. He's living just over in Friendship, right across the bay. He's been there for the past fifteen years."

"He's—"

"I just came from seeing him."

"You—"

"He wants to see you."

She didn't say anything for the longest time, and Annie realized that she was crying.

"I know it's a surprise after all these years." Annie snatched a few tissues from the box on Lilly's end table and pressed them into her hand. "Do you think you'd like to see him?"

Lilly lowered her head, pressing the tissues to her mouth, trembling with silent sobs.

"Lilly?" Annie squeezed her shaking shoulders. "Are you all right? You're not having trouble breathing again, are you?"

Lilly lifted her head, eyes bright with tears but a determined smile on her face.

"No. No, of course not. I'm fine. I'm sorry for being so silly. Of course I'm fine. I just didn't think that, after all these years, he would still be alive. I just can't quite believe it yet."

Annie smiled and squeezed her shoulders once more. "It's amazing isn't it? And he looked for you. For a long time, he did."

"He would." She shook her head, tearing up again. "It's exactly what he would do. I guess that's partly why I was sure he had been killed all those years ago. He was too good to be true. He still is."

"He's real," Annie assured her. "I talked to him myself. He wants to see you."

"What happened to him? Why didn't he come home after the war?"

"It's … complicated. Once he enlisted, he convinced them to let him do some work behind German lines."

Lilly smiled unsteadily. "He always wanted to."

"It seems there was an explosion of some kind at a munitions factory he was supposed to sabotage. He doesn't know what happened exactly, but afterward he couldn't remember who he was. The Germans assumed, since he was wearing one of their uniforms and spoke German, that he was one of theirs. Naturally, they thought he was who he was pretending to be and took care of him."

She put one trembling hand to her lips. "Oh, my poor Peter. Was he badly hurt?"

"He lost the hearing in one ear and has a bad knee. That's all. But it took him almost twenty years to remember who he really was. By then, the Berlin Wall had been built, he was in East Germany, and he couldn't get back. Not until the Wall came down, and the Army brought him back to the States. They gave him the Purple Heart."

Lilly beamed, teary-eyed.

"I suppose you didn't always get all the news while you were in Guam," Annie said, "or you'd have heard about it back then."

Lilly dabbed her eyes with a tissue. "When was it?"

"1992. Almost fifty years after he enlisted. It's pretty amazing."

"I guess it was good that I didn't know about it. It might have been ... awkward with Jimmy and everything. Peter knew him too. Did he tell you that?"

Annie only smiled. "Yes. And I remember him mentioning someone called Jimmy in one of the letters you left with Gram."

"He always used to tease me about Jimmy running away with me," Lilly admitted, laughing faintly. "Funny I ended up marrying him after all."

Annie squeezed her hand. "You know what Peter told me about that? He said Jimmy was a good man, and he was glad you had someone to take care of you when he couldn't."

Lilly dabbed her eyes again. "That's Peter, through and through."

"Once he got back to the States, he tried for a long time to find you, but you having a different last name and living out of the country made it hard for him."

"I guess—" Lilly sighed. "I guess we just weren't meant to be."

"Then, maybe," Annie offered. "But what about now?"

"Now?"

"He wants to see you."

Lilly smiled at that and then slowly shook her head.

"Of course he does," Annie said. "You know he does."

"I'm sure he told you that." Lilly blotted her face with her tissue and sat up straighter in her chair. "As I said, it's exactly what he would do—keep his promise."

"Well, then, tell me when you want to see him, and I'll let him know. Or would you rather call him? He gave me his number."

"No. I don't want to call him."

Annie nodded. "Then when would you like him to—"

"I don't want to call him," Lilly said. "I don't want to write him. I don't want to see him. I buried Peter Lambert seventy years ago. It's too late to bring him back now."

"But he *is* back. He's just a few miles away, and he wants very much to see you."

"No, dear. He doesn't."

Annie let out a frustrated sigh. "I don't understand."

"He doesn't want to see *me*." She opened the drawer in the end table beside her couch and took out a framed photograph. "He wants to see *her*."

The picture was the steely black and white of the 1940s. It showed a girl in a full-skirted white sundress standing in what must have been someone's front yard. She had one gloved hand atop her head, holding on her wide-brimmed hat. Annie recognized the sweet heart-shaped face. It was Lilly.

"Oh, what a beautiful picture."

Lilly smiled a little. "I never used to like having my picture taken. I always thought I was too skinny and too gawky looking. Ah, well, youth is wasted on the young."

"You were lovely then, and you're lovely now." Annie nodded. "Truly."

Lilly grinned unsteadily. "Liar. I have a mirror, you know."

Annie smiled and took a deep breath. "Peter's not eighteen

anymore either, in case you're wondering. And he'd look a little funny strolling around town with a teenage girl on his arm."

Lilly laughed, and then the tears came back into her eyes. "I can't meet him. I just can't. He's not going to be the boy I remember. I'm not going to be the girl he's been looking for all these years. Nineteen forty-three was a long, long time ago. We've both changed."

"I guess so," Annie said. "There's nothing anybody can do about that. But maybe ...."

Lilly turned her head to one side. "Maybe what?"

"Maybe he's somebody you'd like to meet now." Annie let a twinkle come into her eyes. "He's still a charmer, I can tell you that."

Lilly laughed softly. "That's Peter all right. And the funny thing is, he never even knew the effect he had on people. I guess that was part of what made him so attractive."

Annie laughed too. "How about you give it some thought then? You don't have to decide right this minute. I'm sure all this is a lot to take in." She dug in her purse and took out a little scrap of paper. "If you decide you want to see him or talk to him, here's his number. Just think about it."

Lilly looked at the paper for a long time. Then she pressed her lips together. "No. It's no use. I'm not going to see him. I'd rather remember him the way he was, and I'd rather he remember me the way I was." She stuffed the paper back into Annie's hand. "Tell him I have the fondest memories of him, but I really can't see him."

Annie didn't say anything. She had told Carl she wouldn't try to press his mother into anything she didn't want to do. But poor Peter. Everything Annie had found out about him showed he had never wavered in his devotion to Lilly. After seventy long years, he was still determined to keep his promise to her.

Annie sighed. "I'll hang onto it then. If you decide you want to talk to him after all, give me a call."

Lilly twisted her delicate fingers together, looking as if she might at any moment burst into tears. "You—you understand, don't you?"

"I'm trying to understand, Lilly." Annie gave her a sympathetic smile. "It's been a long time since you've seen him. You'd both have a lot of memories and expectations after so long. Of course you're afraid. I suppose he is too—at least a little."

Lilly shook her head, helplessly. "It's just too much. I can't even imagine it now, even though I used to dream of it every night."

Annie squeezed her hand, the little slip of paper crackling between them. "Really, Lilly, it's all right. I don't want you to feel pressured into doing anything you don't want to do. And I'm sure he wouldn't want you to be either. He's a good and patient man. And something that's becoming rarer every day, he's a gentleman. He would never want to make you uncomfortable."

A tear rolled down her withered cheek. "Oh, Peter, Peter."

Annie slipped one arm around Lilly's shoulders. "I know it's a lot to take in all at once. You don't have to decide anything right this minute."

"No. I may be a foolish old woman, but I'm not going to be that foolish. Peter and I, we remember each other at our best. Why spoil that for either of us?"

"I'll tell him then."

Annie wished now that she had never found Peter at all. She wished she had never met him and that she hadn't taken such a liking to him. She hated even the thought of disappointing him. But it was out of her control. She was only the messenger. She could just pray that either she would see Lilly's way was best or that Lilly would have a change of heart. Love freely given was such a precious thing. How sad to see it needlessly rejected. And such ageless faithfulness.

She smoothed the slip of paper with Peter's phone number on it and tucked it back into her purse. It would keep. After seventy long years, a few days more or less wouldn't matter. Once again she gave Lilly a brief hug.

"Please don't worry about this. You're the only one who knows what's right for you. I'll take care of things with Peter."

Lilly nodded, eyes brimming with tears. "Tell him I'm sorry."

Annie wanted to cry as she got back into her car, but she only took out her phone again and called Peter.

"Well, Annie! I didn't expect to hear from you so soon."

She could hear the smile in his voice and picture the warmth in his blue eyes. She hated to extinguish it.

"Would it be all right if I came back to see you right now, Peter? I need to tell you something."

"Sure, I guess. Where are you?"

Annie sighed. "I'm in Bremen, but I could be at your apartment in just a few minutes."

He hesitated. "You've been to see Lilly, haven't you?"

"I'm sorry, Peter." Annie took a deep breath and tried

to sound a little brighter. "I hope she'll change her mind in time. I'm sure she will."

"She won't see me?"

"No. I'm afraid not."

"Not even for a minute or two?"

Annie shook her head and then, realizing he couldn't see that over the phone, cleared her suddenly tight throat. "No. I'm so sorry."

"Not even a telephone call?"

Annie squeezed her eyes shut, wishing there was some other answer to give him. "I'm sorry. No."

"Did—Did she say why? Was it something I did?"

His voice was steady, even stoic, but there was such a note of sadness in it, the tears sprang again to Annie's eyes.

"No," she said, trying to hide the catch in her voice. "No, not at all. I'm sure she'd never want you to think that. She just thinks it's too late now. She thinks you both should remember the way things were and leave it at that."

Peter had no answer for that.

"I'm sorry," she whispered when the silence became unbearable. "I'm really sorry I even stirred all this up."

He didn't say anything for a few seconds, and then he sighed. "Don't even think that, Annie. If nothing else, you set my mind at ease letting me know my Lilly has had a good and happy life, and that she's always been loved and cared for. That was my biggest worry all these years, and now I know for certain. It's a huge favor—a gift, really—and I thank you for it." Again he was silent for a while. "Do you think I could at least send her a note?"

"I—I don't know. Her son was pretty firm about you

not contacting her if she didn't want you to. I wouldn't feel comfortable giving you that, but I know you could probably find it on your own, if you want to."

"What if I give it to you and you pass it on? I promise I won't go looking for her."

"I don't know how that could be a problem," Annie said. "You write your note, and I'll come by and pick it up."

"Really? It's not too much trouble?"

"It's the least I can do."

*   *   *   *

When Annie came back to Lilly's apartment with the note, she found Lilly sitting there where she had left her. Obviously she had been crying the whole time.

"Lilly," Annie murmured, hurrying to her. "I'm so sorry to have upset you."

Lilly shook her head. "It's not your fault. You only meant to help, and I asked you to find out what you could."

Annie sat beside her again and put her arm around her. "But I never meant it to make you unhappy."

Lilly didn't say anything, and Annie finally retrieved Peter's note from her purse.

"He sent you this."

"You went to see him again?"

Annie nodded. "I told him what you said, and he asked if he could at least write. I thought, in case you didn't want him to know where you were, that I'd better just bring it to you. I hope that's OK."

She handed Lilly the note. For a long time, Lilly only sat

staring at the envelope. The only thing written on it was her name in a strong, rather old-fashioned–looking script. The same script that was on the letters Lilly had cherished for more than seventy years.

"That's his writing. I'd know it anywhere even now."

A tear fell onto her name, and she quickly blotted it away. Then, with a pleading glance at Annie, she opened the envelope and unfolded the paper inside. For a long time she stared at it. Then she wiped her glasses and stared again. Finally, she handed the note to Annie.

"Please, I can't even see to read." Lilly laughed. "At this point, you know more about both of us than we do about each other. I don't think there's anything in there you can't see."

Annie opened the note, took a deep breath and began to read. "'My dearest Lilly, I was sorry to hear that you don't want to see me. I'm sure you must have your reasons for that, but I can't figure out what they might be. I ask nothing of you, Lil.'" Annie looked up to see that Lilly had her eyes squeezed shut, and then she continued reading. "'I know it's been seventy years since we last saw each other. Can it possibly have been *that* long? But it seems it has. I know you married and had a fine family. I even peeked in on your latest addition the other day. I happened to catch a glimpse of the baby's mother too, when I was at the hospital.'"

Lilly caught her breath. "He saw little Lilly?"

"I hope you don't mind," Annie said with the tiniest of smiles. "I wanted to go see her, and I didn't think it would hurt anything if Peter saw her too. She's gorgeous."

Lilly beamed. "Isn't she? I'm glad Peter got to see

her. And Callie." She took a deep breath. "What else does he say?"

Annie turned back to the note. "'I happened to catch a glimpse of the baby's mother too, when I was at the hospital. She's a lot like you were before the war. I could almost see you again when she came down that corridor. I know we're strangers now. Perhaps we've missed our time, and it's too late to go back. But I can't help thinking that can't be right. We meant too much to each other once for us to not spare each other a few minutes. I was hoping you'd at least let me keep my promise to come back to you, even if it is just to say hello.'"

She glanced again at Lilly. She had her head down again, shaking it slightly.

"Peter, Peter," she whispered. "I'm so sorry."

"Please don't feel bad." Annie reached over and took her delicate hand. "He doesn't want you to feel bad. Not for his sake. He's not like that."

"I know. I know, and that's what makes me feel so bad. After all that's happened, he hasn't been anything but true to me, and I—"

"You did exactly what he wanted you to do." Annie squeezed her hand. "Listen to what else he says. 'I was hoping you'd at least let me keep my promise to come back to you, even if it is just to say hello. But that doesn't matter. I know now that you had the family you always wanted and that you were well cared for. I know you kept your promise to me to move on if I didn't come back. Thank you for that. With all my heart, I pray God will bless you. Peter.'"

Annie looked up, tears in her own eyes as she handed the note back to Lilly.

Lilly only shook her head. "No! No, no, no. He's just as stubborn and idealistic as he's always been. I'm not that girl anymore. He's not—"

"Maybe he is. Maybe he *is* still that boy. Inside." Annie hugged her one last time before she stood to go. "At least think about it."

"You again."

Annie stopped where she was. She hadn't heard the door open. Obviously neither had Lilly. Annie struggled to make her expression a little more pleasant as she turned to face Lilly's daughter-in-law.

"Marsha, dear." Lilly patted the chair beside her. "Come and sit down for a while. I didn't think you'd be by today."

"Hello, Marsha," Annie said, smiling politely.

"I guess it's a good thing I dropped by." Marsha came into the room, but did not accept the chair Lilly offered her. "You aren't planning on taking up with that Peter Lambert person, are you, Lilly?"

"Well, I—"

"Carl told me all about him. He says you haven't seen him since the war. That was a very long time ago. What in the world could he want after all this time?"

Lilly glanced up at Annie, and Annie gave her a supportive smile.

"We were planning on getting married once the war was over." Lilly said finally. "Circumstances ... changed, and I married Carl's dad instead. I'm sure Peter just wants to say hello now. It's not anything that should worry you."

"Maybe you don't think so. But a lot of elderly people are taken advantage of by men like this. I just want you to be careful."

Lilly only pressed her lips together in response, and no one said anything for a long moment.

"Maybe I'd better go," Annie said finally.

"You probably should," Marsha said. "I really need to have a talk with my mother-in-law. A private talk."

Annie looked at Lilly, waiting to see whether or not she wanted her to leave. Lilly only looked miserable for a moment and then smiled weakly.

"Maybe you should, honey. We'll talk again soon."

Annie nodded. "All right. But you call me if you need anything." Annie glared at Marsha, who was looking at her in sour triumph. "Anything at all. Anytime."

Annie gave Lilly a brief hug and then got her purse and went out to her car.

Marsha was right behind her.

— 17 —

"Just a minute!"

Annie stopped there on the sidewalk outside Lilly's apartment and turned at Marsha's stern voice. "Yes?"

"I don't know how many times I have to tell you this, Annie Dawson, but I really don't want you upsetting Lilly or bringing up things from her past. All that is over now. And to tell you the truth, I don't trust this Peter Lambert. I don't doubt that he knows Lilly has a little money. No wonder he rushed up to the hospital when she was there. He didn't want her dying before he got hold of some of her cash."

Annie waited patiently for her to finish. Then she smiled. "I'm sure Lilly is perfectly able to decide who she wants to see and who she doesn't. Just because she's reached a certain age doesn't mean she's incompetent."

Marsha pursed her lips. "It doesn't mean she's not foolish either. Carl told me about this man. Lilly's been dreaming of him for seventy years. It's ridiculous."

"It's very sweet, if you ask me. And pretty amazing too, that they have loved and remembered each other so long." Annie smiled slightly. "Do you know what Peter told me? Even when he couldn't remember who he was, he remembered he belonged to someone. He knew there was someone out there he loved, someone he had made promises to. If it makes the two of them happy to finally get back together again and talk about old times, who does that hurt? As you say, she's been dreaming of him for seventy years. And he's been waiting to come back to her all that time. Why stand in their way?"

"Because it's foolishness. For goodness sake, she's nearly eighty-eight years old."

"And that means she doesn't have a heart anymore? That she can't still love someone?" Annie lifted her chin. "Just what is the cutoff date for romance? And who said you were the one who gets to decide when that is?"

"Look, Mrs. Dawson, you've known my mother-in-law for a very short time. I don't know where you get off acting like you know what's best for her."

"Nobody would have to know her long to see that she's perfectly capable of making her own decisions. Especially about who she spends her time with."

Marsha put one hand on her hip, her head cocked to one side. "You mean she's perfectly capable of being taken advantage of by this man. You know nothing about him besides what he's told you. Why in the world should we risk having him suddenly back in Lilly's life?"

"I guess that's her risk to take, not yours," Annie said, her voice low and cool. "Lilly's an adult. She's still allowed to run her own life, isn't she?"

"Ruin her own life, you mean."

"What exactly do you have against Peter?" Annie asked. "He just wants to talk to her."

"Yes, it'll start that way. Then pretty soon they'll be spending time together, to 'talk about old times.' And then they'll start dating, if you can call it that at their age. And finally he'll want her to marry him. And then you know what happens."

"What? They live happily ever after?"

Marsha's eyes flashed. "If she dies first, he inherits everything she has. Her family, her real family, gets nothing. It's not right, I tell you. We're the ones who have looked after her all this time, and for him to just waltz in and take everything—"

"Oh, please." Annie had to force herself not to laugh. "Is that all you can see here? The money?"

"It happens, Annie. My father remarried after my mother died. He was seventy-two and 'in love.'" Marsha snorted. "When he died without a will four months later, his thirty-five-year-old wife got everything he had. She remarried six weeks after that. So you can probably guess what I think of the idea of eternal devotion between my mother-in-law and this man she hasn't seen in seventy years."

Annie couldn't help feeling sorry for her. She had obviously been letting this issue fester for a long time now.

"Marsha, I'm sorry. I really am. But you know what? Whatever property your father had when he died was his, not yours. If he didn't have a will, then you don't know what he wanted done with everything. I know you must have been disappointed, but that's just the way it is sometimes. If that woman made your dad happy, then maybe you should try being glad about that instead of letting the whole situation make you bitter." Annie's expression softened. "Besides, aren't you getting a little ahead of yourself? Lilly and Peter haven't even laid eyes on each other in seventy years, and you've already got them at the altar. Maybe all they want to do is talk. Maybe by now they won't even be able to stand each other."

"Well, you can think that all you want. I'm not as naïve as you are. And I'm going to make sure my family is protected. I'm sure Peter would lose interest pretty quickly if he found out that all Lilly's money was in trust, and she couldn't spend any of it without our approval."

"What do you mean?"

"If Carl and I were made her guardians, then she wouldn't be quite so attractive to fortune hunters, would she?"

"Oh, that's ridiculous." Annie shook her head and dug her keys out of her purse. "Anybody can see that Lilly is perfectly competent to take care of her own affairs. And I can't imagine Carl would play along with something like that—just because she might want to talk to Peter?"

"Carl told me what his father did," Marsha said, a superior little smirk on her face. "He doesn't want his mother to know what his father did."

Annie's eyes widened. "You wouldn't."

"Not if he cooperates with me about this. And I'm sure he would."

Annie was speechless. She could tell just from the few times she had talked with him that Carl loved his mother and was very protective of her. But how much did he let his wife bully him? Surely he wouldn't let her convince him to do anything to hurt Lilly.

Annie clutched her keys a little more tightly. "I know I'm not family, but I'm going to keep an eye on Lilly. If you try to do anything, I'll make sure you won't get away with it.

Lilly's very sweet, and I can see she doesn't always speak up for herself around you, but that doesn't mean other people won't speak for her."

Without another word, Annie got into her car and drove away. All during the drive back home, Annie fumed over what Marsha had said. How dare she treat her own mother-in-law like a backward child? She'd talk to Carl about this if Marsha dared to do anything. She'd get Ian to make some kind of official inquiry. She ... well, she didn't know exactly what she'd do, but she'd do something. At her age, Lilly deserved to be treated with respect and dignity.

The more Annie thought about it, the more she fumed. When she got back to Stony Point, instead of taking Ocean Drive to Grey Gables, she drove over to Ian's house. She'd talk to him about this now, if he was home. Yes, his blue pickup was parked in front. She parked her Malibu next to his truck and knocked on the door.

"Annie!" Ian smiled as he opened the door and invited her in. "What is it today? Requests? Accolades? Complaints? Stony Point's mayor is always at your service."

She smiled reluctantly. How did he always manage to make her feel better? "I was just hoping you had a minute to talk."

"Sure. Have a seat."

He turned off the television, and they both sat down on the couch.

"Now, before we discuss anything else, I have to know something." His smile was hopeful. "Are you still going to the banquet with me?"

She laughed. "Of course. I did give my solemn oath."

"Whew." He wiped the pretend sweat from his brow. "I feel better. Now what did you come to talk about?"

"I'm afraid it's Lilly again."

"What now? Is Carl still being difficult?"

"No, actually. I finally got him to meet with Peter and me. He agreed that I could tell Lilly that Peter is alive."

"That's great."

Annie sighed. "Well, it is, and it isn't. I told her about Peter, and she says she doesn't want to see him."

Ian's mouth dropped open. "You're kidding me. Why?"

"Cold feet, I think. She thinks he's expecting her to look like she did seventy years ago. But I think mostly she's just scared. She's dreamed of him all these years, and now he's actually real. I can understand how that could be pretty intimidating for her."

"That's a shame. It really is. I feel bad for Peter."

"Me too, Ian. I think he must be the nicest guy I've ever met."

He grinned. "Besides me, you mean."

"Oh, present company excepted, of course," she said with a laugh, but then she sobered again. "But this is what I came to see you about. Remember Marsha, Lilly's daughter-in-law? I think I told you about her."

"Definitely."

"She's pretty set against Lilly ever seeing Peter again, even for a few minutes. She has some crazy idea that Peter is after Lilly's money."

Ian knit his brow. "Seriously?"

"She told me in no uncertain terms that she wasn't

going to let Peter get his hands on Lilly's money, even if she and Carl had to have her declared incompetent."

"Lilly's not, is she? Incompetent, I mean."

"No more than I am. I tell you, it's crazy. Marsha can't do something like that, can she?"

Ian pressed his lips together, dark eyes flashing. "I guess she can try, but I don't think she'd be successful. Incompetency procedures are pretty complicated, especially when an obviously competent person is fighting it. Besides, Carl wouldn't let her, would he?"

"That's what bothers me. I don't think he would, but she seems like she can be really difficult when she wants to be. Maybe he just wouldn't stand up to her. I don't know."

"Look, I don't want you to worry about all this." Ian held out his arms. "Come here."

She gave him a reluctant little smile, but then she slid across the couch and into his strong, warm arms.

"I can tell you care about what happens to Lilly. I know how much you like Peter. But I don't want you to worry about all of this. We'll keep an eye on Lilly. Besides, if Lilly has already decided she doesn't want to see Peter, then there's nothing to worry about, right?"

She frowned, and he hugged her a little more tightly.

"Right?"

She laughed, blushing faintly. "Right.

Something Alice had said came back to her all of a sudden. *Don't let being afraid spoil something that could be really good.* What exactly was she afraid of? What people might say? That it wouldn't be the same as it had been with Wayne? Of course it wouldn't be the same. Wayne and Ian

were not the same. Even she was not the same as she had
been when she had first met Wayne. It wouldn't be the same.
It couldn't be the same. But could it be as good?

She leaned into the hug, closing her eyes and letting
herself just enjoy the moment. How good his arms felt
around her again, safe and warm, but she couldn't help feeling a little something more, something that made her heart
beat a little faster, something that made her skin tingle. She
could get used to this.

He sighed softly, and she could feel his breath in her
hair, but he didn't say anything. He didn't move. He just
held her there, close but not confining, and after a moment
she lifted her head from his shoulder and grazed her lips
against his cheek.

"Thank you, Ian. For—for just being there for me."
Then she kissed him, warmly and gently. Without another
word she pulled away, stood up and hurried out to her car.

*   *   *   *

The next couple of days were filled with preparations for
the banquet. Annie and the ladies from the Hook and Needle
Club spent Good Friday setting up the tables in the fellowship hall and ironing out last-minute details. She was happily
exhausted when she came home late in the afternoon to find
Boots complaining vociferously over her empty bowl.

"What did you do all day, Miss Boots? Just eat?"

The cat rubbed against Annie's legs, making little
purring meows as Annie poured out some fresh crunchies.
Then Annie went back into the living room to see if she

had any phone messages. Before she could retrieve them, the phone rang.

"Hello?"

"Hello, Annie? This is Lilly Bergstrom."

"Lilly." Annie smiled as she sat down on her couch and kicked off her shoes. "How are you? I've been worried about you ever since I was at your apartment last."

"I'm doing well actually."

Lilly's voice sounded a little shaky, or maybe breathless was a better word for it, but she sounded excited rather than upset.

"I was wondering …."

She didn't say anything for a long moment, and Annie began to wonder if their connection had been lost.

"Lilly?"

Annie heard her take a deep breath.

"I was wondering if you would give someone a message for me."

Annie's lips turned up in a hopeful smile. "Yes?"

"I was wondering if you would tell Peter that I'll be at the Easter banquet on Sunday, and if he still wants to come, I'd really like to talk to him."

"Oh, Lilly! I'm so happy. Of course he'll want to come. I asked him to come, but he wasn't sure he ought to. He didn't want you to feel uncomfortable about coming yourself. But I'm sure if he knows you want to see him, there's nothing that could keep him away."

"I hope so," Lilly said, and her voice was very soft. "Do you think he'll still like me?"

Annie was surprised to feel tears spring into her own

eyes at the uncertain little question. "Of course he will. He loves you already. And he couldn't possibly help liking you." She paused for a moment more, wondering if she ought to even ask, but she just had to know. "Lilly?"

"Yes?"

"What made you change your mind?"

Lilly's sweet laugh rang out. "Marsha. The dear thing, she spent half an hour haranguing me about not seeing him ever again. I felt like a naughty teenage girl being scolded over her crush on a boy from the wrong side of the tracks. And after a while, I realized I rather liked feeling that way. I liked feeling as if I wasn't finished living."

Annie laughed too, imagining how deflating it must have been for Marsha to know her bullying had such an effect. "Good for you!"

"She kept telling me all the reasons I ought not to see Peter again, and they all reminded me why I should. Oh, Annie, she told me—"

Annie bit her lip, suspecting what Lilly was going to say and hating the anguish in her trembling voice.

"What?" Annie asked finally.

"Oh, poor Peter," Lilly cried. "Annie, my husband knew. Jimmy knew Peter was alive right after the war. If only I'd known. I could have—"

"You couldn't have done anything about it, Lilly. You couldn't have. Peter didn't even know who he was for almost another twenty years. He wouldn't have known you. And your husband couldn't have known about the amnesia. He even had second thoughts about it being Peter. If he had told you about seeing Peter back then, what would you have done? Your heart would have been broken, wondering why Peter didn't come home—wondering why he chose to stay away."

For a long time, there was only silence on the other end of the line.

"Lilly?" Annie ventured finally. "Are you still there?"

"Yes." Her voice was soft and not very strong. "I'm here."

"You would never have married Jimmy. You wouldn't have lived all over the world and had all the good times you had. You wouldn't have had your kids or your grandkids or your great-grandkids. And what about little Lilly, that new great-great-grandbaby of yours?"

Lilly chuckled faintly. "Well, there is all of that."

"Please, Lilly, don't beat yourself up over something that can't be changed. I know it's terrible that it happened the way it did. I know you would have wanted Peter to come home and for the two of you to have married and started a family together. For whatever reason, it didn't work out that way. Don't let the past spoil the future for you."

"No." Annie could hear the smile in her voice. "No, and that's really why I decided to talk to Peter after all; it wasn't just to get under Marsha's skin. If there's still something there, I want to know it. I'm still a little bit afraid, of course."

"You shouldn't be." Annie couldn't help smiling, even though she knew Lilly couldn't see it. "He's really a wonderful man. And he's waited so long to see you."

"I know. I know." She sighed, but it was a happy, excited sort of sound. "Oh, I feel like I'm planning to go on my very first date."

"You'll do fine," Annie assured her. "If you heard him

talk about you, you'd know you don't have to do anything but be yourself. That's who he wants to see."

"Oh, dear." There was a little tremor in Lilly's voice. "I can't believe I'm actually doing this. What if …?"

"No. Now you have to stop that right there. You can't worry about what ifs. It's not like you're promising to marry him or anything. You're just renewing an acquaintance with an old friend. It will be all right. And I know that, if you don't, you'll always wonder what might have been."

"I suppose you're right." Lilly laughed faintly. "Well, I've decided to go to the banquet. If he wants to come, I'll be there."

Annie couldn't help the grin that spread over her face. "I'll tell him."

— 18 —

Easter morning turned out to be beautiful. The sun was shining as if winter had never been, and by the time the church doors opened, the last stubborn remains of the snow were gone. Annie got out of her car and straightened the skirt of the pink dupioni-silk suit she was wearing. It was cut less formally than most suits, so it had a soft, springlike look to it. She felt fresh and crisp wearing it, as if she were as new as the day.

Gwen and John Palmer were standing near the door chatting with Peggy and Wally Carson, and Annie waved to them.

"Good morning."

The quartet smiled and returned the greeting as Annie passed on into the church foyer.

"Ooh, don't you look pretty?" Alice came up beside her, taking her arm. "Did you get the gravy taken care of? I love Betsy's recipe."

"All taken care of," Annie assured her. "And you won't believe it. After practically tearing that whole attic apart, I finally found Gram's Easter linens. I brought them over when Peggy, Gwen, and I were setting up yesterday."

"Well, it's about time. Where were they?"

Annie grinned, blushing. "In my linen closet."

They both laughed, and then Annie turned Alice a little to one side, looking her over.

"I love that spring green on you. It's just right with your eyes."

Alice made a brief pirouette. "Thank you. Shoes dyed especially to match." She flicked her pearl earrings. "And, of course, Princessa."

Annie grinned. "Lovely."

They walked toward the sanctuary and found Mary Beth and Kate near the doors, both in their Easter best. They all exchanged hugs.

"Another of your creations, I see," Annie told Kate, admiring the fine robin's egg blue yarn of her crocheted jacket. "That's gorgeous."

Kate blushed faintly, and Mary Beth beamed at her. "She's a walking advertisement for the shop. I should pay her even on Sundays."

"Oh, good. I'm glad you're all together." Stella hurried up to them with Peggy and Gwen in tow. "We all need to sit toward the back of the church. When Reverend Wallace has everyone stand for the closing prayer, we can slip out and start getting everything ready for the banquet."

"I had a quick peek this morning, and everything you set up yesterday looks great," Stella said. "The fellowship hall is beautiful."

"I just love your grandmother's linens," Gwen told Annie. "I'm so glad you finally found them. The whole Easter 'dinner at Grandma's' idea is just wonderful. It's really like going home."

"It's been a lot of work," Annie said, "but I think it's turned out well. It's going to be fun."

"Good morning."

Ian glanced around at the group, smiling as he walked up. But his eyes were on Annie. She returned his smile shyly.

"Good morning, Ian. How are you?"

"It's a beautiful day, and I'm surrounded by beautiful ladies," he said. "I couldn't be better. Are we all ready to go in?"

Peggy and Gwen saw that their husbands were waiting for them. Annie took the arm Ian offered her, and they all went into the sanctuary, sitting in the back.

By the time the service started, the pews were full. Reverend Wallace opened the service with a prayer, and just as the first hymn began, the sanctuary door opened once again.

Annie glanced over and caught her breath. Peter Lambert gave her a nod and a smile as he slipped into the back pew, dapper in a dark blue suit and crisp white shirt. She squeezed Ian's hand and nodded toward Peter. Seeing him, Ian grinned at her, and then they joined in the hymn.

The song service concluded, Reverend Wallace began his Easter sermon. Annie always loved hearing the story of Christ's love that led Him to lay down His life and of His glorious resurrection. It was about life springing from death—about hope where there was no hope. It was about a promise being kept when it seemed impossible that it would ever be. Easter was a time of new beginnings and fresh starts, no matter what had gone before. And as she glanced again at Peter who was following along with the Easter story in his well-worn Bible, Annie couldn't help but think what this particular Easter might mean to Lilly Pryce Bergstrom.

But there was no Lilly. As the service neared its conclusion, Annie realized that Lilly must have decided that the past was simply too difficult to rise above.

"She didn't come," Annie said, as she and Alice walked behind the rest of the Hook and Needle Club members through the foyer of the church and headed toward the fellowship hall. "I'm so disappointed."

Alice gave her a sympathetic nod. "I hope that doesn't mean she's chickening out on the banquet too. After everything that's happened, it would be such a shame. And was that who I think it was in the back pew there?"

Annie grinned. "Yes, that's Peter. Isn't he great? I've about half fallen in love with him myself."

"Ooh, you'd better not let Ian hear you say that."

Annie's face turned hot. "Oh, hush."

"Just what are you going to do about Ian?"

Annie shrugged.

Alice made a face. "I know, I know. You don't know. If Lilly chickens out, I won't be able to say much about it. Both of you—you're just alike. You have wonderful guys who love you dearly, and you don't know what to do about them. You act like real love just grows on trees or something. *Harrumph!*"

Annie laughed at her melodramatic expression. "You should have been an actress. Now come on before everyone else gets to do all the work."

They hurried after the others, but Annie knew Alice hadn't just been teasing her. Maybe if Lilly didn't chicken out, Annie wouldn't either.

For a while, Annie was too busy to think of lost loves or new beginnings. There were all the little things that never failed to pop up at the last minute. Finally, just before they opened the doors, Annie stood looking at the fellowship hall. It was beautiful. The big tables were covered with homemade tablecloths and a variety of vintage dishes, and little accent antiques were scattered around. There were arrangements of Easter lilies set up on the serving tables, and everything looked quaint and cozy. It truly was like Easter dinner at Grandma's house. And better than the sight was the smell.

Annie closed her eyes and breathed in the fragrance of ham and turkey and homemade rolls.

"What do you think? Do we pass inspection?" Mary Beth asked.

Annie opened her eyes and smiled. "With flying colors. It's glorious." She gave a questioning look to the other ladies who had gathered to admire their hard work. "Well, are we ready?"

Alice nodded, and Peggy hurried over and threw open the doors.

"Come and get it!"

Quickly the room filled with chatter and laughter as the people lined up at the serving tables. Annie smiled to see Ian and Peter come in together, evidently deep in conversation.

"You two look like you're up to no good," she observed, taking them each by an arm.

Ian waggled his eyebrows at her, making her laugh, but Peter's brave attempt at a smile came up a little bit short.

"Do you suppose she'll come?" he asked. "I didn't see her in the service."

She squeezed his arm a little more tightly. "Lilly said she'd be here. I'm sure, unless there's really some emergency, she will be. Don't worry. Why don't you two get in line and enjoy yourselves for now? I have some work to do, but save me a seat." She looked at Ian. "Promise?"

"Sure. After all, you gave your official oath." He pretended to be stern, but his dark eyes twinkled. "And I'm sure there's at least one statute on the books about not standing up the town mayor. Could be some pretty stern penalties involved."

Annie laughed, patting his arm before she released it. "I'll try to stay on the straight and narrow, at least for today. See you in a few minutes."

She hurried over to her station beside Alice at the serving line just in time to hear the authoritative clink of a butter knife against a water glass. Reverend Wallace cleared his throat.

"We're so pleased to have all of you with us today," he said, "whether you are part of our regular church family or are just visiting. Either way, we are all family in the eyes of the Lord, and at His table all are welcome. If you would, please bow your heads." He bowed his own head and closed his eyes, reverently asking the blessing. Afterward, there was a chorus of "Amen," and Reverend Wallace smiled. "Let's eat!"

Once everyone was served, Annie filled her own plate and sat down with Ian. She noticed that his food and Peter's was still untouched.

"You should have eaten. It'll all be cold by now."

"I didn't want you to have to eat alone," Ian said. "We both know that's no fun."

Peter glanced toward the door and then down at his plate. "I was still hoping for an Easter miracle, but maybe it's too late." He picked up his knife and fork, and cut himself a bite of turkey, but before his fork reached his mouth, Annie put her hand on his arm.

"No. Not too late at all."

Peter looked toward the door again. There was Carl Bergstrom in his Sunday best, and on his arm, radiant in a daisy-fresh white dress, was Lilly.

* * * *

Lilly stood there in the doorway, searching the fellowship hall, wondering exactly what she was expecting to see. Then she held on to her son's arm a little more tightly.

"Maybe this wasn't such a good idea."

"We've been all through this, Mom." Carl's eyes were warm. "If it makes you happy, it makes me happy."

"But about your dad—"

"We both know Dad loved you. I'm sorry I never honored his last wish. I should have told you long before now. Maybe things would have turned out differently."

She shook her head when she saw Annie sitting at a table under one of the windows. Annie was beaming at Lilly, whose gaze now fell upon the man who was walking toward her. Trembling, Lilly smiled up at her son. "Maybe things were meant to be just like this."

She recognized Peter at once. He was still lean and tall, even if not quite so tall as he had been. But he stood straight, and despite the cane, his steps were still firm and sure. The gold of his hair had turned to silver, but it was still thick, cut as it had been before the war, before the

Army had shorn it almost to nothing. His eyes were still the piercing blue she remembered, the blue of the sky and of the shirt he had worn to the enlistment office.

He knew her too. She knew she had changed, that she had grayed, wrinkled, and sagged, but he knew her. And he didn't turn away. Eyes lit, he smiled, that smile that crinkled the corners of his eyes, and she knew it was him. Not just Peter Lambert, but *her* Peter, the one she had always loved, the one who'd left her seventy—no, it couldn't be seventy years ago. He was old, and she was old, but they were still the Peter and Lilly who had fallen in love despite the madness of a world at war.

He was old. He was changed. That couldn't be helped, but would he still have that genuine sweetness she remembered? Would he still have that inborn nobility and simplicity she had fallen in love with?

"Lilly."

That was all he said, and though his voice was a bit thin, it was the one she had kept in her memories, in her dreams, in her heart. And if it quavered more than a little, maybe that was explained more by the tears in his eyes than the lines on his face.

"Lilly."

Carl grinned and slipped his arm out of her grasp. "You're in good hands, Mom. I'm going to get us both some lunch."

The two men exchanged an understanding nod, and then Carl hurried toward the serving tables. Peter only smiled at her still, and then he took her hand, his grip gentle but firm.

"May I?"

The seventeen-year-old Lilly smiled inside her, painting her withered cheeks with a girlish blush, and she nodded. He was still a gentleman even after all these years.

He touched his lips to her hand, his eyes warmly locked on hers, and before she knew it she was in his arms.

"Oh, Peter, Peter," she sobbed against his shoulder, amazed he somehow still had that fresh-laundry smell she remembered so well. "Is it really you?"

He laughed softly and leaned his cheek against her hair. "It's me, Lil. I have a few more miles on me than the last time I saw you, but it's me." She felt a slight tremor run though him, and then the lightest touch of his lips against her hair. "I'm so sorry. I'm sorry it's taken me so long to get home to you."

"It's a miracle," she whispered. "An Easter miracle."

He gave her another strong hug and then pulled back from her, looking her up and down. "You're still the best-looking woman in the room."

She laughed up at him, and still holding on to her hand, he offered her his arm.

"May I?" he asked once again.

"Of course."

She settled her arm in his, amazed how it felt so natural there, even after all the years that had passed. He turned them toward the table where Annie and several others sat, and then he looked at her again.

"You know, we could go back and sit at the table with everyone else. Or ..." He nodded toward a couple of overstuffed chairs on either side of a little end table in the corner.

She smiled and nodded, and he led her to one of the chairs and helped her into it. Then he sat down beside her.

"Now," he said with a sigh of contentment. "Now I've really kept my promise."

She looked into his eyes—Peter's eyes, she knew—the same eyes that had caught her young heart in those innocent days before the war. Before either of them could say a word, Carl was standing in front of them, two generously filled plates in his hands.

"I thought you two would probably rather talk than eat. This way you can do both."

"Thanks, son," Lilly told him.

Peter gave him a nod. "Thank you, Carl."

Lilly knew he was thanking her son for more than just the food.

"Are you happy, Mom?"

There was a tender, searching look on Carl's face, and when Lilly nodded through the tears that brimmed in her eyes, he smiled.

"I guess you two have a lot to catch up on, huh? I'll be over at the table. If you need anything, either of you, just let me know."

"You raised a good man there, Lil," Peter told her, squeezing her hand a little more tightly.

"I think so. But I might be a little biased." She smiled, still not quite believing she was talking to Peter, *her* Peter, at last. "I guess we *do* have a lot of catching up to do."

He shot her that easy smile she had never forgotten. "Seems to me that I promised you once that, when we were old and gray, I'd tell you all my hair-raising adventures."

She felt a warm glow steal over her, and she couldn't help but remember the very first kiss they had shared when 1943 was brand-new. "I'd like that."

"Might take a while to tell you about them all."

Her lashes dropped shyly to her cheeks. "I'd like that even better."

*   *   *   *

Carl nudged Annie. He had taken the seat next to her, the one Peter had vacated. "Look at Mom. I haven't seen her this happy since before Dad died."

Annie smiled at him. "Evidently your wife helped her make up her mind about seeing Peter again."

"Yeah, Marsha can be a handful," Carl said, giving her a rueful little smile in return. "She told me she lit into you too. I'm sorry."

Annie shrugged. "I can take it. I just didn't want her to upset your mother."

"Yeah, well, Marsha's dad kind of jumped the traces when her mother died. She's more than a little bitter about it. I wasn't too happy to know she told Mom that Dad knew that Mr. Lambert was alive right after the war. But it sounds like Mom took it like a champ."

"Yes, she did," Annie agreed.

"It's kinda hard for me to say this to you, Annie," Carl said soberly, "especially after some of the rough things I said to you. Thank you for making this happen. Thank you for Mom's happiness. Thank you for pushing me to do the right thing, even when I wanted to hide from it." Breaking the seriousness of the moment, Carl stood up. "I understand you ladies make a mean buttermilk pie and that I'd better get some before it's gone."

Annie laughed. "Better hurry."

She watched him as he headed toward the dessert table, and then she looked over at Lilly and Peter again, the two of them glowing like teenagers as they sat and talked, and she couldn't help thinking of the poem by Robert Browning:

Grow old along with me!
The best is yet to be,
The last of life, for which the first was made:
Our times are in His hand
Who saith "A whole I planned,
Youth shows but half; trust God: see all nor be afraid!"

Truly, youth was only the beginning of God's plan for life. It would be so sad to imagine there was nothing more. Annie certainly could tell there was more for Lilly and Peter, even though they had outlived most of their peers. Their bodies had aged, but not their hearts, and that was a miracle in itself.

There was something very endearing about the couple, something strong and unbreakable—something that said they belonged together. And it seemed particularly appropriate that they would be brought together again at Easter, a time of renewed hope and life.

"Nice, huh?"

Annie looked up to see Ian smiling at her. She smiled too.

"Yes, it's very nice." She shook her head. "Look at them. You'd think they hadn't been apart at all during those seventy years."

His eyes were warm. "Do you suppose they'll get married at last?"

Annie laughed. "It's a little early to expect that, I think. After so long, I suppose they have a lot of things to talk about. Still, it wouldn't surprise me if they did one day. They're both delightful people, and they've waited so long. It wouldn't surprise me in the least."

Ian looked at her, and after a moment's hesitation, took her hand in his. "Some folks are just meant to be together."

"Yes." She squeezed his hand a little and then smiled into his eyes. "I think they are."

He bit his lip, hesitating again. "And what about us, Annie? Are you going to make me wait seventy years?"

She looked at their joined hands and then, again, up into his face. Finally she looked over at the lovebirds once more. They were laughing now, and it was a lovely sound.

"No." She felt a little shy, but all at once she felt a rush of excitement. *The best is yet to be.* Blushing, she looked across at Ian. "Well, certainly not seventy years."

Ian smiled, and they laughed together intimately, just like Peter and Lilly.

Learn more about Annie's fiction books at

AnniesFiction.com

- Access your e-books
- Discover exciting new series
- Read sample chapters
- Watch video book trailers
- Share your feedback

We've designed the Annie's Fiction website especially for you!

Plus, manage your account online!

- Check your account status
- Make payments online
- Update your address

Visit us at AnniesFiction.com